THE GOOD EVIL

NITHIN RAPHY

For those who have faced betrayal at the hands of those they
trusted the most
and chose not to let the darkness consume them.

To the broken boys who became warriors.
To the silent screams that never found a voice.
To every soul that carries the weight of the past and still dares to
fight for the future.

This story is for you.

— Nithin Raphy

Contents

Preface

This book is a work of fiction. All characters, places, organizations, and events portrayed in this story are products of the author's imagination. Any similarities to actual persons, living or dead, or to real-life events are purely coincidental and unintentional.

The story does not intend to reflect or represent any real group, ideology, religion, or belief system. Any references that appear familiar are coincidental and should not be interpreted otherwise.

This is a creative work meant for storytelling and emotional exploration. Reader discretion is advised.

Acknowledgements

To the readers, whether you're holding this book out of curiosity or connection, thank you. You are the heartbeat that brings these pages to life.

To the people who inspire my characters, some real, some imagined, your essence lives between the lines. Thank you for showing me that even the most broken people can carry the most beautiful stories.

To those who reminded me, gently or forcefully, to never give up, I heard you.

Lastly, to every silent survivor of grief, pain, or pasts they rarely speak of, this one is for you. May you find pieces of yourself in these words, and may they remind you that healing is not linear, but it is possible.

Foreword

Some stories begin with love.
Some with loss.
This one begins with both, and the destruction that follows when love is betrayed.

The Good Evil is not just a tale of vengeance or survival. It is a journey through grief, identity, and the blurred line between right and wrong. At its core, this story asks one haunting question: What happens to the boy who is left behind when everything he loves is taken away?

Ayan's journey is raw, intense, and uncomfortable at times, but it is also necessary. Because in a world where silence often follows trauma, his voice, however broken, deserves to be heard.

As the author, I did not write this book to glorify violence or darkness. I wrote it to explore what happens when pain goes unspoken for too long, when anger becomes armor, and when the people meant to protect us become the very ones we must survive.

If you have ever carried the weight of your past like a second skin, or struggled to reconcile the person you were with the person you are becoming, then this story might echo with you.

Thank you for picking up this book.
Thank you for stepping into Ayan's world.
And above all, thank you for listening.
— Nithin Raphy

ONE

THE BEGINNING OF THE END

Mumbai, October 7, 2004.

The clock struck 3:00 PM.

Ayan's eyes were fixed on the slow-moving second hand, its rhythmic ticking drowning out the muffled sounds of pencils scratching against paper. His fingers drummed lightly on the desk. "One more hour to go."

Today wasn't just any day. It was his father's birthday, and the house would be filled with family: uncles, aunts, and cousins. The thought made his heart race with excitement. But before he could join them, he had to sit through the final hour of his exam.

He hadn't touched his paper in a while. Instead, he just sat there, staring at the clock, wishing time would move faster.

A sharp tap on his desk snapped him back to reality.

"Ayan, why are your eyes not on your paper?"

It was Sister Josephine, the strictest instructor in school. A woman whose sharp gaze alone was enough to keep even the most mischievous students in line. She never went anywhere without her wooden ruler, tapping it against her palm as she watched over the students.

Ayan turned to her, unfazed.

"I'm already done, ma'am."

Sister Josephine's eyebrows lifted slightly before she nodded.

"I'm not surprised. The Yusuf Ali family only produces geniuses." She paused, then added, "But keep your focus on the sheet, Ayan. You need to work even harder if you ever want to catch up with your older brother."

Ayan's grip on his pencil tightened slightly.

Kabir Yusuf Ali.

His fifteen-year-old brother, the school's golden boy. He had been Student of the Year three years in a row, excelling in everything: academics, sports, and debates. Teachers still spoke of him with admiration, and students still compared themselves to him.

Ayan sometimes felt the weight of those expectations pressing down on him. But more than that, he loved Kabir. Admired him. Worshipped him.

Kabir had been everything to him: his guide, his mentor, his best friend. He taught Ayan how to solve the toughest math problems, helped him perfect his cricket stance, and told him stories before bed. Kabir was the best brother in the world.

At least, he used to be.

Lately, Kabir had been distant. He barely spoke to Ayan anymore. Whenever Ayan asked him to play or help with schoolwork, Kabir always had an excuse…"I'm busy," "Maybe later," "Not now."

Ayan tried to brush it off. Maybe that's just what happens when you grow up. Maybe older kids had more responsibilities.

But deep down, he missed his brother.

He let out a quiet sigh and turned towards the window. Outside, the afternoon sun bathed the schoolyard in golden light. The trees stood still, not a single leaf rustling.

The world outside seemed unnaturally quiet.
Too quiet.

Ayan exhaled, a strange unease settling in his chest.

It's a calm day.
Way too calm.

The bell finally rang.

Ayan shot up from his seat, slinging his bag over his shoulder as students rushed out of the classroom. His heart pounded with excitement. Home. Family. Celebration.

He dashed down the school steps, weaving through the crowd of children chattering about their holiday plans. His driver was already waiting by the gate. Ayan climbed into the bus, barely able to sit still.

As the vehicle rumbled through the city streets, he imagined the scene at home: his mother's warm hug, the aroma of biryani filling the air, his father laughing with guests, Kabir waiting for him at the door. Everything would be perfect.

But when they turned into his neighborhood, something felt... off.

The street was eerily silent.

Ayan's house stood at the end of the lane, a grand two-story home that usually gleamed under the sun. But today, the front gate was open, and the door, slightly ajar.

A sinking feeling coiled in his stomach.

"Stop the bus," Ayan said.

He stepped inside. His shoes tapped softly against the marble floor. The scent of biryani and sweets still lingered in the air, but there was something else, something metallic. A sharp, bitter smell that made his stomach turn.

His heart pounded as he moved deeper inside.

The house had always been filled with warmth, with laughter. But now, an eerie stillness suffocated the air.

A plate lay shattered on the floor near the dining table, food spilled across the tiles. A faint creak echoed through the silence as a curtain swayed slightly, as if someone had just passed through.

Ayan swallowed hard. His throat was dry.

Then he saw it.

Aunt Farida's body lay motionless in the hallway. Her eyes, wide and lifeless, stared at the ceiling, her mouth slightly open as if frozen mid-scream. Blood pooled beneath her, dark and thick, soaking into the rug.

Ayan froze. His breath caught in his throat.

This wasn't real. It couldn't be real.

His feet moved on their own, carrying him forward. His small hands trembled as he gripped the edge of the doorway and peered inside the living room.

His uncle. His cousins.

People he had just seen that morning, laughing, talking, were now sprawled across the floor, their bodies twisted unnaturally. Blood smeared the furniture, the walls, and the once-pristine carpet. A tea set lay overturned beside his uncle's outstretched hand, the porcelain stained crimson.

Ayan's tiny fingers dug into the doorframe. His chest rose and fell in sharp, ragged breaths.

He wanted to scream.

But no sound came out.

His gaze drifted across the room, and then he saw him.

Kabir Yusuf Ali.

Standing near their parents' lifeless bodies.

His white kurta was drenched in red. In his grip, a kitchen knife gleamed under the dim light, its blade dripping thick, fresh blood.

Ayan's vision blurred. His head spun.

"...Bhai?" His voice was barely above a whisper. A plea. A desperate hope that his brother, the one who had always protected him, would explain. Would tell him this wasn't real.

Kabir tilted his head slightly, his dark eyes unreadable.

For the first time in Ayan's life, his brother's gaze felt like that of a stranger.

Then, Kabir spoke. His voice was calm. Emotionless.

"Foolish brother, I killed them."

Ayan's stomach lurched. His ears rang.

"Whaat? Wh...Why? Why would you?"

Kabir's grip tightened around the knife. His lips curled slightly, almost like a smirk.

"They made me weak," Kabir said, without a shred of remorse.

"They didn't want a son. They wanted a product. A trophy. Everything was conditional: love, pride, even a meal at the table. Be a doctor. Be obedient. Be perfect. And when I cracked under it, they didn't ask why… they asked what more I could give. So I did. I gave them everything. Even their deaths."

He glanced down at their parents' bodies. Their mother's saree was still neat, her gold bangles smeared with red. Their father's hand was frozen mid-reach, as if he had tried to grab something, or someone.

Kabir continued, his voice eerily steady.

"Now, I am free. Free to live as I want. I finally feel powerful."

Ayan's small frame shook violently.

"You… you're lying."

His voice cracked. His tiny fists clenched at his sides.

Kabir ignored him.

Without a second thought, he reached down and yanked the gold chain from their mother's neck. The clasp snapped. He pocketed it casually, as if it meant nothing.

Ayan staggered back. His stomach twisted.

This wasn't his brother.

This couldn't be his Kabir.

Kabir turned to leave. But before he did, he paused beside Ayan.

Slowly, deliberately, he wiped the bloodied knife on Ayan's shoulder, staining his school uniform.

Ayan flinched. His breath hitched as Kabir leaned in, his voice a cold whisper against his ear.

"You are not even worth killing, weak bastard."

Ayan collapsed onto the floor. His knees buckled, his vision darkening at the edges. His heart pounded so hard it hurt.

His world spun. His mind screamed, but his body refused to move.

The last thing he heard before everything went black was the sound of Kabir's footsteps fading away.

TWO

THE GUARDIAN

Ayan woke up in a hospital bed two days later, his body weak, his mind lost in the haze of trauma. The first thing he saw when he opened his eyes was the concerned face of Commissioner Raghav Murthi.

The 45-year-old police officer had been by his side ever since the incident. He had seen countless crime scenes in his career, but nothing had prepared him for the horror of the Yusuf Ali massacre. Yet, amidst the bloodshed, the sight of the unconscious boy lying on the floor had affected him the most.

Raghav had lost his wife and two children in the line of duty ten years ago. He knew what it meant to have everything taken away in an instant. He saw the same emptiness in Ayan's eyes, the same unbearable grief he had once felt.

As Ayan stirred, confusion flickered in his gaze. Panic set in as memories of that night flooded back.

"Bhai..." he murmured weakly, his small fingers gripping the hospital sheet.

"Shh... you are safe now, beta," Raghav said gently, placing a reassuring hand on Ayan's shoulder.

But Ayan didn't feel safe. Not anymore.

In the days that followed, Raghav made a decision. Ayan had no one left in the world, and he needed guidance. Raghav, who had spent years drowning in his own loneliness, saw a purpose in the broken boy. He decided to take Ayan under his wings, not just out of pity but because he knew the boy needed more than just a home. He needed someone to show him a path forward.

Thus began a new chapter in Ayan's life, under the wing of a man who understood his pain all too well.
But one thing never changed. Ayan had only one goal: to find Kabir and kill him.

The weeks that followed were filled with silence.

Living with Raghav was quiet. The house was spacious and calm, but Ayan remained distant, never quite letting his guard down. Sometimes, Raghav's old friend from the army, Balveer Singh, would visit. They often sat in Raghav's study, doors half-shut, having hushed conversations that never piqued Ayan's curiosity. Balveer had tried, in the beginning, bringing toys, cracking jokes, and offering gifts. But Ayan's silence stayed firm. Eventually, even Balveer stopped trying. Their interactions became limited to polite nods and soft-spoken greetings, just a "Hi Ayan" or "How are you?" before fading into the background like everything else.

Ayan moved through the days like a ghost, speaking only when necessary, barely acknowledging anyone around him. He spent most of his time staring out the window of Raghav's house, watching the world go on as if nothing had happened. His food remained untouched on the table, growing cold with each passing meal. His body weakened, but he didn't care. Sleep was scarce. Every time he closed his eyes, he saw blood, heard Kabir's voice, and felt the weight of that night pressing down on him. When exhaustion finally forced him into slumber, he would wake up drenched in sweat, gasping for air.

Raghav tried to talk to him, but Ayan never responded. The warmth of the new home meant nothing; the kindness in Raghav's voice felt distant. Every sound, every shadow, every fleeting moment reminded him of what he had lost. The emptiness inside him only grew heavier.

And then, one night, he couldn't take it anymore.

Slipping out of bed, he quietly left Raghav's house and made his way back to the only place he had ever known as home.

Standing outside the Yusuf Ali residence, Ayan felt a lump form in his throat. The house was dark and abandoned, its windows cracked, its walls stained with memories. His feet felt rooted to the ground as he looked up at the balcony where his mother used to call him inside for dinner. He turned his gaze to the front door, half-expecting it to swing open and reveal her standing there with a warm smile.

But there was nothing. Just silence.

Tears blurred his vision as he stepped forward, his hands trembling as he pushed open the door. The house smelled of dust and decay, but in his mind, he could still remember the scent of his mother's cooking and the distant laughter of his family echoing through the halls.

A sob caught in his throat as he took cautious steps inside. His gaze darted around the living room, his heart pounding. Maybe they're still here... maybe it was all just a bad dream...

Then, a noise from the kitchen shattered the silence.

Ayan's breath hitched. His body reacted before his mind could process, and he ran towards the sound. "Mom!" he cried out, desperation coating his voice.

As he turned the corner, his heart slammed against his chest.

A steel glass lay on the floor, rolling in slow circles. A cat, startled by his sudden entrance, dashed out through the broken window.

His legs gave out, and he sank to the cold floor. His fingers dug into the tiles as sobs wracked his small frame. He wasn't sure how long he stayed there, drowning in grief, unable to breathe past the ache in his chest.

Then, a warm hand rested on his shoulder.

Raghav had found him.

Without saying a word, Raghav knelt beside him and pulled him into his arms. Ayan didn't resist. He let himself be held, even as his body trembled. For the first time since that night, he felt something other than emptiness. Pain, yes, but also something else. Something like warmth.

As he held the grieving child, Raghav's own past came rushing back. He saw himself in Ayan, in the way he clung to sorrow like a lifeline. He recalled the night he had collapsed in the very same way, holding his wife and two daughters after they had been taken from him.

Pain recognized pain. And in that moment, Raghav silently vowed that Ayan would not have to face his alone.

As time passed, Ayan decided to return to school. He knew if he wanted to take revenge, he needed to learn and get stronger. The school was the first step to escaping weakness.

The first few weeks were unbearable. Whispers followed him through the hallways, hushed voices speaking of the "boy whose family was murdered." Some students stared, and others avoided him entirely. The teachers were gentle with him, too gentle, as if one wrong word would shatter him. Ayan hated it.

He stopped taking the school bus, instead chose to walk home. The long walk gave him time to be alone with his thoughts, to escape the pitying looks and murmurs.

One day, as he turned a familiar corner, he froze.

A figure stood at a distance.

Kabir.

Before Ayan could react, the figure was gone.

Shaking his head, he forced himself to walk forward. I must be hallucinating...

THREE

THE WEIGHT OF WEAKNESS

Ayan had always been alone, but school made his loneliness feel suffocating. He had learned to ignore the whispers and stares at school, but some things were impossible to ignore.

Manav Sharma was one of them.

A senior student, tall and fat, Manav walked through the corridors like he owned them, always surrounded by his lackeys. He enjoyed making life miserable for those smaller or weaker than him. And Ayan, with his withdrawn nature and quiet demeanor, had quickly become his favorite target.

It started with small things: bumping into him in the hallway, knocking his books to the floor, muttering insults under his breath. Ayan did nothing. He clenched his fists, gritted his teeth, and endured it. But the more he endured, the worse it got.

At lunch, he could hear the murmurs from other students.

"That's the kid from the massacre house..."

"I heard his brother is a murderer."

"Creepy, isn't he? Always so quiet."

Ayan sat alone, staring at his untouched food, forcing himself not to react. But every whisper, every stolen glance, chipped away at his patience.

He hated it.

Not just the stares, not just the whispers. He hated himself for feeling so powerless.

The Breaking Point

One evening, as Ayan walked home alone, following his usual routine to escape the prying eyes at school, he heard footsteps behind him.

He ignored them at first, but the voices soon followed.

"Oi, orphan boy!"

Ayan's steps slowed, his grip tightening around the strap of his bag. He knew that voice.

Manav and his friends.

He turned into a quieter alley, hoping they would lose interest. They didn't.

A hand clamped onto his shoulder and yanked him back.

"Think you're too good to talk to us, huh?" Manav sneered. His friends laughed, circling Ayan like vultures.

Ayan clenched his jaw. He had endured enough.

Without thinking, he swung his fist toward Manav's face.

It was a mistake.

The punch was weak and untrained. It barely made Manav flinch. Instead, it made him grin.

"Oh? You've got some fight in you, orphan boy?" His amusement faded as he cracked his knuckles. "Let's see how much."

Before Ayan could react, Manav's fist slammed into his stomach, knocking the wind out of him. Another punch landed on his cheek. A kick sent him sprawling to the ground.

He curled up, protecting his face as the blows rained down.

By the time they left, laughing and mocking him, Ayan's body ached all over. His lip was split, and bruises were already forming on his arms and ribs.

He forced himself up and stumbled home.

Raghav was waiting when Ayan walked through the door. The moment he saw the bruises, his expression darkened.

"What happened?" His voice was calm but firm.

Ayan wiped his bleeding lip with the back of his hand. "I fell down."

Raghav didn't respond. He just stood there, watching.

Ayan couldn't meet his gaze. He knew Raghav didn't believe him, but the older man didn't press further.

"Go wash up," Raghav finally said, with a calm tone.

Ayan nodded and walked away, relieved that the conversation was over. What he didn't know was that Raghav already had the truth. His teacher had called earlier, informing him of the bullying incident.

That night, as Ayan lay in bed, staring at the ceiling, he heard the sound of Raghav's footsteps outside his room.

But the door never opened.

And the footsteps eventually faded away.

The following morning, Raghav had assigned an officer to discreetly watch over Ayan. The moment Manav and his group approached again, the officer intervened. With a sharp warning, the bullies scattered.

But when Ayan saw this, he became furious.

"You think I need a babysitter?!" he snapped at Raghav that evening. "You don't have to protect me like I'm some lost puppy!"

"Ayan...

"If I can't even stand up to a bully, how the hell will I ever face that devil?!" Ayan's voice cracked with frustration.

Raghav opened his mouth to respond, but Ayan didn't wait. He turned on his heels, stormed into his room, and slammed the door shut.

That night, untouched plates sat cold on the table, and silence filled the spaces where words should have been.

The next morning, Raghav woke Ayan early. It was a Saturday, and instead of their usual routine, he drove Ayan across the city.

They pulled up in front of a large, well-maintained building with a sign that read Varghese Martial Arts Academy.

Ayan frowned. "What is this?"

"Your first step toward strength." Raghav got out of the car, motioning for Ayan to follow.

Inside the academy, students practiced under the watchful eye of a tall, well-built man in a black karate gi. His stance was strong, his movements precise, exuding an aura of discipline and power. He turned toward them as they entered, his sharp eyes assessing Ayan in an instant.

"Tom Varghese," Raghav introduced. "6th Dan Black Belt. One of the best martial artists in the city. He's going to train you."

Tom folded his arms. "So, you're the kid?"

Ayan hesitated. "Yeah."

Tom smirked. "We'll see if you have what it takes."

Ayan didn't know what awaited him in that academy, but one thing was certain: he would never be weak again.

Ayan threw himself into training with relentless determination. Under Tom's strict but effective guidance, he learned discipline, endurance, and the art of combat. Every strike, every block, and every stance drilled into him carried the weight of his resolve.

The bruises from his past beatings faded, replaced by hardened muscle and sharpened instincts. Though he rarely spoke, his actions spoke volumes. His teachers noticed the change. Ayan was more focused, and his academic performance improved alongside his physical strength. He wasn't just surviving; he was transforming.

The bullies, too, noticed the change. Whispers spread through the school that Ayan was no longer an easy target. Some dismissed it as a rumor, but Manav and his gang learned the truth the hard way.

One evening, as Ayan walked home, they cornered him again. But this time, he wasn't afraid. When Manav lunged at him, Ayan sidestepped effortlessly, driving his fist into Manav's gut with precision. The once-feared bully crumpled to the ground, gasping for air. His lackeys hesitated, exchanging nervous glances before deciding they wanted no part of this fight.

From that day on, Ayan was no longer just the orphan boy. He was respected by his peers, feared by his bullies, and silently acknowledged by those who once whispered behind his back.

Yet, for Ayan, this was just the beginning. Strength was not just about winning fights; it was about preparing for the one battle that truly mattered.

FOUR

The Weight of Revenge

Pain became routine.

At school, Ayan was nothing more than an easy target. The taunts, the shoves, the fists, they came daily, but he no longer reacted. He let the blows land. Let his body absorb the pain. Each time he hit the ground, he stood back up. He never fought back, never spoke a word.

And in some twisted way, it made him feel stronger.

At first, every punch and kick hurt like fire searing his skin. But over time, the pain dulled. His body hardened. He stopped flinching. The bruises stopped mattering. The aches in his ribs and the cuts on his lips were nothing compared to what burned inside him.

At the academy, he trained. He trained until his muscles screamed, until his body felt like it would collapse. Tom was relentless, pushing him beyond his limits. Every strike he learned, every fall he took, was another piece of armor forged onto him. He still felt weak, but he knew he was getting stronger.

Months passed.

And then, the day came.

The school hallway was loud as usual, filled with students laughing and chatting, but Ayan barely heard any of it. He walked with his head down, his hands in his pockets, lost in thought. Until he felt a familiar shove against his shoulder.

He barely stumbled.

"Oi, orphan boy!" Manav's voice dripped with amusement. "Ignoring me now?"

Ayan didn't respond.

"Tch. Did you go deaf or what? What, did your new daddy teach you some manners?" Manav sneered, stepping in front of him.

Ayan looked up.

Something in his gaze made Manav hesitate. Just for a second.

Then he laughed. "Look at you. Acting all tough. But you're still the same weak little..."

Ayan caught the punch.

Gasps rippled through the hallway.

For the first time, Ayan wasn't on the ground. He wasn't bleeding. He wasn't taking it. He was standing. And he wasn't letting go.

Manav's wrist trembled under Ayan's grip. His friends stood frozen, waiting for the usual outcome: for Ayan to back down, to run, to break.

But Ayan didn't. He met Manav's eyes, his voice steady.

"Now my turn."

The first punch landed hard, knocking Manav back. The second hit even harder.

Panic spread through the group. Someone screamed. Someone ran. But Manav had no time to react. Ayan moved too fast, too precise. His training had sharpened his instincts, turned his rage into something focused. Controlled.

Manav tried to swing back, but it was useless. Ayan dodged, his footwork clean, his fists unrelenting. Another hit to the ribs. Another to the face. Manav stumbled, blood trickling down his nose. His eyes widened with something Ayan had never seen in them before.

Fear.

The last thing Manav saw was Ayan's fist driving into his face one last time before darkness took him.

Ayan stood over his unconscious body, breathing hard, his fists shaking. Blood stained his knuckles, but he felt nothing. No pain. No regret.

For the first time, he felt powerful.

Next Day...

The principal's office was heavy with silence, thick and suffocating like the air before a storm. The rain outside tapped against the windows in an erratic rhythm, the only sound in the room aside from the distant murmurs of students in the hall. The weight of what had happened settled over everyone present, but no one spoke first.

Principal Mehra sat behind his polished desk, his hands clasped tightly together, his expression weary. On the other side, Mr. Sharma stood rigid, his anger barely restrained. His face was red with frustration, his breathing uneven as he paced back and forth, his shoes tapping against the wooden floor with sharp, deliberate steps.

"My son is in the ICU," Mr. Sharma finally broke the silence, his voice sharp and laced with fury. "And you're sitting here, asking me to be patient?" His eyes flicked between Principal Mehra and Raghav before settling on Ayan, who sat still and unbothered, his gaze fixed downward. His knuckles were slightly bruised, a faint mark still visible on his cheek, but otherwise, he looked untouched, unaffected, and completely indifferent.

"That boy... Mr. Sharma pointed a shaking finger at Ayan, "Beat my son unconscious! Doctors say he'll live, but do you have any idea what condition he's in? And you expect me to sit here and let this go? I want the police involved! This is assault!"

Principal Mehra took a slow breath, choosing his words carefully. "Mr. Sharma, I understand your anger. This is a serious incident, and I do not take it lightly. But...

"But what?" Mr. Sharma snapped, cutting him off. "You're going to defend him? That violent, unhinged...

Raghav, who had remained silent until now, shifted slightly in his chair. His expression was unreadable, his voice dangerously calm when he spoke. "If a case is filed," he said, "then Manav will be involved just as much as Ayan."

The words sent a chill through the room. Mr. Sharma's jaw tightened.

Raghav leaned forward, his tone unwavering. "Your son has been bullying Ayan for months. Beating him, humiliating him, taunting him. We have witnesses: students and teachers who saw it happen and did nothing." His eyes met Mr. Sharma's without flinching. "If you want to take this to the police, we can. Just to remind you, I am the police, and I know how these cases go. It won't just be Ayan facing consequences."

A thick silence followed.

Mr. Sharma's anger faltered, his expression shifting as he weighed the reality of Raghav's words. He opened his mouth, then closed it again. The fight drained from his face, replaced with reluctant acceptance. He muttered something under his breath before exhaling sharply. "Fine," he spat, running a hand through his hair. "But if he so much as touches my son again..."

"He won't," Raghav assured.

Mr. Sharma let out a frustrated sigh, shaking his head as he stormed out of the office, slamming the door behind him.

The room remained still for a moment, the only sound now was the rain outside.

Principal Mehra turned his attention back to Ayan. He studied the boy carefully: his detached expression, his unwavering posture, the emptiness in his eyes. He had seen students lash out before, but this was different. This wasn't just rage. This was something much colder.

"You are suspended for two weeks," Mehra said finally. "Clear your mind."

Ayan didn't argue. He simply nodded, stood up, and walked out without hesitation.

Once the door closed, Principal Mehra let out a tired sigh and looked at Raghav. "That boy needs help. I strongly suggest taking him to a psychiatrist."

Raghav exhaled slowly, glancing at the rain-speckled window. For a moment, doubt flickered in his mind. Had he made a mistake sending Ayan to the academy? Had he given him strength but failed to teach him control?

But the thought passed just as quickly. This was always going to happen. The anger inside Ayan wasn't something any psychiatrist could fix.

"No psychiatrist can help him right now," Raghav said finally. His voice was quiet but certain. "The only one who can help him... is himself."

FIVE

BURIED TRUTHS

The first few days of Ayan's suspension passed in silence. He spent most of his time alone, either in his room or sitting in the garden, staring at the sky. He barely touched his training equipment, nor did he attempt to pick a fight with Raghav about the forced break. Perhaps he knew he had gone too far with Manav. Perhaps he was tired.

One evening, as the sun dipped behind the horizon, Raghav joined him in the garden, settling into a chair nearby. For a while, neither of them spoke. The rustling leaves and chirping birds filled the silence.

"You wanna hear a story?" Raghav finally spoke. His voice was calm, but there was something heavy beneath it, something Ayan had never heard before.

Ayan glanced at him but remained silent.

"A few years ago, Mumbai was ruled by a man named Raju Bhai," Raghav continued, his voice steady but laced with an underlying tension. "He was the kind of man who thrived in the shadows. Murders, drug trafficking, kidnappings. There was no crime he hadn't touched, no brutality he hadn't ordered."

Ayan frowned slightly, but he remained quiet, listening.

"The police tried for years to catch him," Raghav went on. "We failed. Every time we got close, he slipped through our fingers. He had men everywhere: informants inside our own department, criminals willing to kill for him. People were too scared to testify. He was untouchable."

His fingers curled into fists on his lap, a ghost of past frustration flickering in his eyes.

"But I did it," he said, his voice quieter now. "I caught him."

Ayan's brow furrowed.

"It took two months of careful planning, surveillance, and research. We tracked his movements, followed his men, and studied his habits. And one night, when he least expected it, we struck. A raid in the dead of night. No warning. No escape. We got him."

Ayan could almost picture it: the tension of the mission, the adrenaline rushing through Raghav's veins as he finally closed in on the man Mumbai had feared for so long.

"But men like Raju Bhai... they don't go down quietly." Raghav inhaled sharply. "He was dangerous, but the ones loyal to him? They were worse."

He leaned forward slightly, his elbows resting on his knees. His next words were slower, heavier.

"A week after his arrest, I got a call."

Ayan stiffened.

"They had my wife and my children."

Something in Raghav's voice changed. Ayan could hear it: the way it cracked, just slightly, the way the weight of those words pressed down on him even now, years later.

"They told me to release him. Said if I didn't, they'd kill them." Raghav's fingers twitched slightly, as if recalling the feel of the phone in his grip that night. "I told myself they were bluffing. I had to believe they were bluffing. Raju Bhai was a high-profile criminal. Releasing him wasn't an option."

His voice lowered, barely above a whisper.

"They weren't bluffing."

Ayan felt his stomach drop.

"The next morning, I found them," Raghav continued, his eyes fixed on the ground as if he could still see that day in his mind. "My wife. My two daughters. Gone."

The silence between them felt suffocating.

Ayan opened his mouth, then closed it. What could he possibly say?

"For a long time, I lost control," Raghav admitted. "Every criminal I caught, I unleashed all my rage on them. I didn't care if they were small-time thieves or high-level gangsters. I wanted them all to suffer."

His jaw clenched. "Then one day, in the middle of a raid, I saw a man run. He fit the description of one of Raju Bhai's men, and my vision went red. I cornered him in an alley. He begged. Pleaded. But I didn't hear it. I just saw the men who took my family. I saw their faces on him. I pulled my gun and aimed at his head."

Ayan felt his breath hitch.

"And then... I saw his hands." Raghav exhaled shakily. "He was unarmed. No gun. No knife. Nothing."

The image must have been burned into his mind because when he looked at Ayan, his eyes were distant.

"I almost killed an innocent man," he admitted. "All because of my anger."

Ayan swallowed hard.

"That's what anger does," Raghav said, finally meeting his gaze. "It doesn't make you stronger. It makes you reckless. It makes you blind. If I had pulled that trigger, I would have been no different from the criminals I swore to fight."

He let that sink in before continuing.

"You think you're in control when you fight, but the moment you let rage take over, you become something else. Something dangerous." He paused. "You think Kabir started as a killer? No. He probably started with anger as well. Unchecked, unchallenged anger."

Ayan flinched at the mention of his brother but didn't interrupt.

"You think he had a reason for what he did?" Raghav continued. "Maybe he thought he did. Maybe he told himself he was justified. But in the end, it doesn't matter, because he still crossed the line. And once you cross that line, Ayan, there's no coming back."

Ayan exhaled, his breath slow and measured. He didn't argue. He didn't need to. He understood.

For the next week, he did not train. Instead, he sat outside, watching the birds flit from tree to tree, watching the sky shift colors with the passing hours. He forced himself to slow down, to breathe, to think. He replayed his fight with Manav in his head over and over, analyzing every movement, every decision. He had wanted to hurt him. That was the truth. He hadn't wanted only to stop Manav; he had wanted him to suffer.

And that realization disturbed him.

Then, on the ninth day, while cleaning the house, he noticed something unusual in Raghav's room. The bed's mattress was slightly raised, just enough to reveal the edge of some papers tucked beneath. Curiosity got the best of him. He reached in and pulled them out.

Newspapers.

His fingers trembled as he flipped through them. The first page stopped him cold.

Kabir's face.

His brother was plastered across the front page, the headline screaming at him:

'Serial Killer Strikes Again: Father and Son Murdered in Delhi.'

Ayan's breath hitched. He scanned the article, his heart pounding against his ribs. Kabir had been on a killing spree, with eight people dead in Mumbai and now two more in Delhi: a father and his son.

The paper slipped from his grip.

His vision blurred. His chest tightened, and his breath came in short, sharp gasps. His body felt hot, unbearably so, but his fingers were ice-cold.

Panic surged through him. His legs wobbled, and he collapsed onto the floor.

And then...

A flash.

Kabir stood before him, a wicked grin stretched across his blood-streaked face. A knife in his hand, dripping red. Behind him lay their parents, lifeless.

Kabir tilted his head, locking eyes with him.

And then, he laughed.

A sick, taunting laugh that echoed, growing louder, swallowing everything.

Ayan gasped, snapping back to reality.

Kabir was out there, and he was killing again..

The sun had long set, casting the city in a quiet, golden haze, where shadows stretched and the world seemed to exhale. A police car rolled to a stop near the front porch, its engine humming before falling silent. The door creaked open, and Raghav stepped out, his movements slower than usual. He was exhausted, his shoulders heavy with the weight of a long day. Dark circles framed his eyes, his face lined with fatigue. But there was something else beneath the exhaustion. Something harder. Something resolved.

The driver adjusted his cap. "Good night, sir."

Raghav nodded. "Good night, Bhaskar."

As he shut the door, his gaze lifted toward the house. That's when he saw him.

Ayan sat on the porch, hunched over, his elbows resting on his knees. A single newspaper was clenched tightly in his hands, its edges slightly crumpled from his grip. More papers lay scattered on the ground around him, shifting slightly in the breeze. His face was unreadable at first, but as Raghav stepped closer, he saw it.

Impatience. Fear. Anger.

A storm of emotions clashed within the boy, his breath uneven, his fingers tightening around the newspaper as if it were the only thing holding him together.

Raghav knew immediately.

Ayan had seen it. The thing he had tried so hard to shield himself from.

"What is this?" Ayan's voice broke the silence, sharp and cutting. He lifted the paper, shaking it slightly. "Did you know about this and not tell me?"

Raghav exhaled, his expression unreadable. "Come inside."

Ayan didn't move at first. His chest rose and fell in quick, shallow breaths, his body still coiled with tension. But then, slowly, he stood. He followed Raghav into the house, his footsteps heavier than usual, his mind spinning with questions he wasn't sure he wanted the answers to.

Inside, the air felt thicker. He watched as Raghav set a thick file onto the table before gesturing toward the couch.

"Sit."

Ayan sat, his fists clenched on his knees. His body was rigid, his heart hammering against his ribs. He felt like something was about to change, something irreversible.

Raghav ran a hand over his face, then sighed, as if bracing himself. "We've been trying to track Kabir since the night he left your house." His voice was steady and measured, but there was something heavy beneath it. "We still don't know why he killed your family... and we don't know why he's targeting these people now. But based on what we've gathered, we believe he's been looting from them."

"Looting?" Ayan frowned. "For what?"

Raghav shook his head. "We're not sure yet."

Ayan's frustration built like a slow fire. "So what do you know?"

Raghav leaned forward slightly, his hands clasped together. "The last confirmed sighting we have of him was near Kashmir. And from the way it looks... he's heading toward Pakistan."

Ayan's breath hitched. His fingers dug into his knees. "Pakistan?" The word barely escaped his lips. "Why, why would he go there?"

The question hung in the air.

Then, something stirred in Ayan's memory. Pieces of the past, long ignored, began falling into place.

He leaned back against the couch, his mind reaching for details he had once dismissed.

A few weeks before the massacre.

Late at night.

Ayan had always been a little mischievous, climbing through the tree branch that connected his window to Kabir's room, sneaking in to startle him for fun. That night had been no different. He had crept across the branch, ready to jump in and scare his brother.

But then he heard the voice.

Kabir's voice.

Low. Tense. Speaking into the phone.

Ayan hadn't understood most of it at the time, but certain words had stuck. Words that had sent a strange chill through him even then.

"Terrorists", "Bombs", "Guns".

Suddenly, Kabir's eyes flicked toward the window, and he froze. He had just noticed Ayan sitting on the tree branch, partially hidden by the shadows, watching him. His grip on the phone tightened for a second before he abruptly hung up the call.

His expression shifted, nervous and tense. It wasn't the usual annoyance when Ayan sneaked into his room. This was something sharper, something uncertain.

"What are you doing there?" Kabir's voice was tight, forced. He took a step closer to the window. "Get inside. Now."

Ayan asked. "Bhayya, who were you talking to?"

Kabir's reaction was instant, too instant. His body tensed, and his eyes flickered with something unreadable before settling into sharp irritation. "Why are you sneaking up on me?" he snapped, his voice harsher than Ayan had ever heard before. "Are you spying on my calls now?"

Ayan took a step back, his stomach twisting. He hadn't meant to upset him, but Kabir's sudden anger felt... different. Wrong. "I...I just heard something," Ayan stammered.

Kabir exhaled sharply and ran a hand through his hair. His expression softened just a little when he saw the hurt in Ayan's eyes. Ayan felt a lump rise in his throat, confused and shaken by his brother's reaction. He almost wanted to cry.

Kabir sighed, stepping closer and lowering his voice. "Shh, don't make a big deal out of it. It was just a game. I was giving my friend some tips on how to play. That's all." He placed a hand on Ayan's head, ruffling his hair like he always did when trying to reassure him. "Nothing serious. Just a stupid game."

Ayan had believed him.

Until now.

He swallowed hard and forced himself to meet Raghav's gaze. Slowly, he repeated the memory, word for word.

Raghav didn't react the way Ayan expected. There was no shock, no wide-eyed disbelief. Instead, for a brief second, something flickered in his expression, something restrained. He was choosing his words carefully.

After a long pause, he finally spoke.

"It's as we feared, Ayan." His voice was quiet but firm. "It seems Kabir had connections with a terrorist group. And I think he's heading to them now... to escape from us."

Ayan's body locked up. His breath grew shallow.

His mind screamed at him to reject it, to fight it, to claim it wasn't true.

But the pieces fit.

The phone calls. The words. The massacre.

The brother who had carried him on his shoulders. Who had protected him, laughed with him, and prayed with him. The one who had held his hand when he was scared, who had promised to always be there.

Not only was he a murderer. Not only had he wiped out their entire family.

But now... now he was something worse.

Now, Kabir was the enemy of the nation.

A terrorist.

The word tore through Ayan's soul, hollowing out something deep inside him. He wanted to scream. To deny it. But all he could do was sit there, frozen, as the weight of that truth crashed over him like an unforgiving wave.

Days turned into weeks. Weeks turned into months. Ayan never returned to his old school after the two-week suspension. Both he and Raghav knew it was impossible. The weight of being the Ayan Yusuf Ali...the brother of a terrorist, would follow him in those hallways. Whispers, stares, judgment. And on top of that, the boy he had put in the hospital. The atmosphere wouldn't let him study, wouldn't let him grow.

So, Raghav made the decision. A new school. A new name.

Ayan Yusuf Ali became Ayan Ali.

Here, no one knew his past. No one knew his family. And he preferred it that way. He kept his head down, spoke to no one, and focused only on studying. The fewer attachments, the better.

At the same time, he continued his martial arts training. Tom personally arranged for him to train under Aditya Choudhary, a strict but disciplined instructor who didn't just teach him how to fight but how to control his anger. How to strengthen his body without letting his emotions rule him. Ayan excelled.

Raghav allowed him to stay alone, 50 kilometers away, in a hostel near his new school. Ayan agreed and also kept an agreement that Ayan should visit Raghav on weekends. And that was the extent of his connections.

His life became routine, mechanical.

From his room to the academy. From the academy to school. From school back to his room.

No friends. No bonds. No interactions with the world. Just a constant cycle, moving forward, but never truly living.

Meanwhile, the Hunt for Kabir Continued

While Ayan buried himself in routine, the world outside was not as still. Kabir's name echoed through the walls of police stations, his face appeared on countless wanted posters, and his presence was whispered among criminals who feared him as much as the authorities chasing him.

Raghav and his team worked tirelessly, following every lead, but Kabir was always one step ahead. There were reports, fleeting and unreliable, of him being seen in different parts of the country. A grainy CCTV capture at a railway station in Jaipur. A witness in Amritsar, swearing he saw a man matching Kabir's description disappear into the crowd. A stolen vehicle abandoned near the Kashmir border, blood staining the driver's seat, but no body.

There were bodies, though. A small-time smuggler in Delhi, found with his throat slit. A businessman in Punjab, murdered in his home, and his safe was emptied. And in every case, the evidence was circumstantial, the connection to Kabir frustratingly unclear. Was he simply looting to survive, or was there something more?

One night, a captured informant whispered a name, a contact Kabir had supposedly met before vanishing again. But before he could reveal more, he was found dead in his holding cell. Strangled. No security footage, no signs of forced entry. Just silence.

The pattern was unmistakable. Kabir wasn't just running; he was moving with purpose, his steps leading him toward something beyond mere survival. And if the trail of bodies meant anything, it was that nothing would stop him.

SIX

AGAINST ALL WALLS

Years passed, and Ayan grew into a quiet, distant young man. Standing at 5.9 feet, with curly hair that framed his sharp features, a well-built body honed from years of training, and a voice edged with quiet intensity, he moved through life like a shadow. His routine was precise and relentless, rigid, predictable, and devoid of any unnecessary distractions.

Every morning, he woke up at 5 AM, his alarm cutting through the silence. A run through the still-dark streets, followed by rigorous training at the martial arts academy, then college. He excelled in academics, absorbing knowledge with the same discipline he applied to his physical training. But beyond his studies and training, there was nothing. No friendships, no attachments. He had built walls too high for anyone to climb.

But at night, Ayan lived a different life. Hidden behind his cupboard, he had built a secret wall filled with newspaper clippings, red strings connecting locations, and notes scribbled in urgency. Every single lead on Kabir. Every missing person's report that matched Kabir's pattern, every murder, every robbery. But Kabir was a ghost. Reports of sightings popped up in Kashmir, then disappeared. Some claimed they saw him in Punjab, others in Nepal. The truth was, no one could track him, not even the police.

And yet, sometimes, when Ayan was alone in his room, he had the eerie feeling that Kabir was near. Watching.

Meanwhile, under Commissioner Raghav's command, the police had successfully thwarted multiple bomb blasts across India. Their sources had uncovered plots in Delhi, Mumbai, and Hyderabad, each one connected to a larger web of terror. Somehow, Kabir's name kept surfacing, even if only in whispers. They had stopped massacres before they happened, dismantled sleeper cells, and intercepted crucial intelligence. But Kabir remained untouchable.

Things remained the same for Ayan till that day!

The day that Siva joined

Siva Malhotra transferred mid-semester into Ayan's class. From the moment he stepped onto campus, he was impossible to ignore. At 5.7 feet, slim, always wearing a denim jacket, and with his ever-present guitar slung over his back, he looked like he belonged on a stage rather than a classroom. He introduced himself with a casual confidence that made people feel like they'd known him for years.

By the end of his first day, Siva had already made friends across different groups. He was the kind of person who could walk into a room full of strangers and leave with a dozen new contacts in his phone. He joked with professors, helped students with assignments he barely understood himself, and charmed his way into every circle.

But there was one person he couldn't figure out.

Ayan.

Everyone in college knew Ayan. He was the best student and the biggest mystery. He never spoke unless necessary, never lingered in conversations, and never showed interest in anything outside his strict routine. He was good-looking but intimidating, his sharp gaze making people hesitate before approaching him. The only thing people knew about him was that he was incredibly disciplined, highly intelligent, and utterly untouchable.

"Don't bother with him," Imtiaz, one of his classmates, warned Siva when he tried to introduce himself. "Ayan doesn't talk to anyone."

Siva raised an eyebrow. "Huh! Doesn't talk to anyone"

That made him more curious.

Siva started watching Ayan, not in a creepy way, but with fascination. He noticed how Ayan's schedule never changed, how he avoided unnecessary eye contact, and how he finished his work with a level of precision most people couldn't achieve. The more Ayan ignored him, the more Siva wanted to talk to him.

The first attempt happened in the canteen.

"Hey, you always this serious, or do you have a secret life as an assassin?" Siva asked, plopping down beside Ayan.

Ayan didn't respond, continuing to eat his food in silence.

Undeterred, Siva drummed his fingers on the table. "Silent types, huh? Mysterious, brooding, loner vibe? You know, girls love that."

Ayan barely spared him a glance.

Siva smirked. "I bet you have a tragic backstory. Maybe you're a lost prince in exile. Or... wait, are you secretly a spy? Oh man, you totally are, aren't you? The whole 'don't talk to anyone' thing? Classic cover."

Ayan exhaled sharply. "Do you ever shut up?"

Siva grinned. "Ah-ha! He speaks! That's progress, my friend."

Ayan sighed and returned to his food, hoping Siva would lose interest. But Siva wasn't the type to give up.

One morning, he decided to take things up a notch. He waited on Ayan's usual route to college, scattered nails on the road, and hid nearby.

As expected, Ayan's Royal Enfield rolled over the nails. A sharp hiss followed. He stopped, inspecting his now-flat tires.

Siva, grinning ear to ear, strolled up. "Wow, man, what are the odds? Looks like you need a ride."

Ayan exhaled sharply. "You did this?"

"Me?!" Siva placed a hand on his chest, feigning shock. "How dare you accuse an innocent bystander of such villainy?"

Ayan folded his arms. "I'll take a cab."

Siva tsked. "Oh, come on. My R15 is right here, ready to save the day. Just hop on."

Ayan glanced at his watch. He was already late, and Ayan hated being late. Begrudgingly, he got on the bike.

As they rode into campus, students stared. Ayan, the brooding loner, was riding behind Siva Malhotra. Siva, being Siva, made sure to take the busiest route, waving at everyone. "Look, ladies and gentlemen! The great Ayan Ali has finally accepted me as his noble steed!"

Ayan resisted the urge to jump off the bike.

When they parked, he got off quickly. "Never again."

Siva smirked. "We'll see about that."

One weekend, as Ayan rode toward Raghav's home, he noticed a familiar figure ahead of him on the road. Siva.

He was riding his R15, weaving through the traffic with his usual effortless confidence. Ayan hadn't expected to see him outside of college. Something about Siva's direction felt unusual. He wasn't heading toward the popular streets or any of the usual hangout spots.

Curious, Ayan slowed his bike and decided to follow him.

The roads became quieter as Siva took a turn off the main street, heading toward an area Ayan had never visited before. The further they went, the fewer cars passed by. Eventually, Siva stopped in front of a small, modest orphanage. The paint on the building was chipped, the walls aged by time, yet it carried a warmth that was undeniable.

Ayan parked his bike at a distance, out of sight, and watched.

Siva greeted a few kids at the gate, ruffling their hair as they cheered his arrival. The moment he stepped inside, more children ran toward him, clinging to his legs, pulling at his hands. He laughed, effortlessly lifting a small boy onto his shoulders, spinning him around as the child squealed in delight.

Then, Siva pulled his guitar from his back and started playing. The children gathered around him, clapping and singing along. His usual carefree energy was still there, but this... this was different. The smile on his face wasn't the playful grin he flashed at college; it was something deeper. Something real.

Ayan had always known Siva as loud, as someone who was constantly surrounded by people, constantly joking, constantly pushing his way into others' lives. But now, watching him here, Ayan saw something else. Someone who wasn't just trying to be liked. Someone who belonged.

For a long moment, Ayan just stood there, watching.

After a while, Siva and the children moved inside. Ayan waited before stepping closer. An older man, dressed in a simple robe, was sweeping the entrance. His movements were slow, unhurried, as if he had seen many days like this one.

Ayan approached. "Siva Malhotra... he comes here often?"

The priest glanced at him, then at the orphanage gates, as if checking to see if Siva was nearby. His gaze settled on Ayan, measuring him before answering.

"Every week," he said finally. "He's been coming for years."

Ayan frowned. Years?

The priest set the broom aside and dusted off his hands. "You're his friend?"

Ayan hesitated. He wasn't sure how to answer that.

Instead, he asked, "Did he... grow up here?"

The priest studied him, his expression unreadable. For a long moment, he said nothing. Then, in a quiet voice, he replied, "Siva does not speak much about the past."

Ayan nodded slowly. He understood that. He understood it too well.

The priest sighed, glancing toward the orphanage doors. "But I will say this... the world was not kind to him when he was young." His voice carried the weight of something unsaid. "Life forced him to stand alone when he should have had a hand to hold."

Ayan's fingers curled slightly. He knew what that felt like.

The priest gave him a small, knowing smile. "But even so, he chooses to bring joy. That is something special, wouldn't you agree?"

Ayan didn't respond. His gaze drifted back to the orphanage, to the sound of laughter spilling from inside. He had never thought of Siva as someone who carried burdens. But now...

He wasn't sure what he thought anymore.

And maybe that was the beginning of something he hadn't expected.

The next day onwards, Ayan started noticing things.

The way Siva always laughed, yet there was something in his eyes that never quite matched.

The way he surrounded himself with people, but never seemed to belong anywhere.

The way he followed Ayan around, not because he wanted something, but because maybe, just maybe, he needed something.

Ayan never asked. Siva never explained.

But one evening, as they sat side by side in the library, Siva humming softly while sketching in his notebook,

Ayan finally muttered, "Do you ever study?" Siva smirked, leaning back in his chair. "Studying is for stupid people. Smart guys like me pass with charm, luck, and last-minute panic."

Ayan exhaled, half amused and half annoyed. "One day, that charm's going to run out."

Siva grinned wider. "Then I'll just borrow some of yours."

Later that night, Ayan left the library late, walking past the dimly lit parking lot, when he heard the familiar strumming of a guitar.

He stopped.

Siva sat on a low wall, plucking the strings of his guitar, the melody soft and unpolished. Ayan didn't recognize the tune, but there was something about the way Siva played, something raw.

"You should head back," Ayan said, his voice quiet. "It's late."

Siva barely glanced up. "So should you."

Ayan exhaled. He had no argument for that.

For a while, neither of them spoke. The music filled the silence between them, unspoken words hiding in the notes.

Then Siva finally asked, "You ever think about taking a break?" Ayan frowned. "From what?"

"Everything." Siva shrugged. "The whole 'serious guy' act. The routine. The training. Just... stopping for a second?"

Ayan's jaw clenched. "I don't have time to waste."

Siva hummed, nodding slowly. "Yeah. I figured you'd say that."

He didn't push. He just kept playing while Ayan turned and walked away.

• 37 •

SEVEN

UNSPOKEN WOUNDS

The evening air was thick with the usual noise of campus life: laughter, chatter, the distant strumming of a guitar from one of the dorm rooms. Ayan walked along the dimly lit courtyard, his mind lost in thought.

He wasn't the type to pay attention to the usual college gossip or conflicts, but something caught his eye near the old chemistry block.

A group of students stood in a semi-circle, whispering among themselves, their expressions a mix of fear and amusement. In the center, a trembling freshman stood against the wall, his back pressed against the cold surface, while Rahul, a well-known bully, loomed over him.

"Look at you," Rahul sneered. "First-year students should know their place. You think you can just walk around here like you own it?"

The boy stammered, trying to speak, but before he could, Rahul shoved him hard against the wall. The spectators chuckled nervously, none of them daring to step in.

Ayan's fingers curled into fists. His instincts kicked in, the same ones that had been driving him since he was a child: the need to punish those who preyed on the weak.

Before he knew it, he had closed the distance.

"Leave him alone."

His voice was calm, but the sharp edge in his tone made the crowd fall silent.

Rahul turned, his cocky smirk unfazed. "Oh, look who it is. The great Ayan, suddenly playing hero?" He scoffed. "Mind your own business, man. This is just fun."

Ayan stepped closer, his piercing gaze locking onto Rahul's. "It doesn't look like fun to me."

Rahul rolled his shoulders, pretending to be unbothered. "What, you wanna fight me over this loser?"

Ayan's patience snapped. In one swift motion, he grabbed Rahul's wrist and twisted it just enough to make him flinch. "Try me."

Rahul winced, struggling against Ayan's iron grip. The smirk vanished from his face. The crowd held their breath, sensing the tension thickening. Ayan was ready to break his arm if it meant teaching him a lesson.

Then, before he could act, a hand rested lightly on his shoulder.

"Ayan," Siva's voice was calm, yet firm.

Ayan didn't turn. His grip tightened slightly, but Siva squeezed his shoulder. His voice dropped to a quiet murmur, but it carried enough weight to cut through the rage burning inside Ayan.

"If you do this, you're not just hitting him...you're becoming someone you swore you'd never be."

The words hit Ayan like a slap.

His grip on Rahul's wrist loosened, and his breath caught in his throat. It was such a simple statement, yet it sent a shockwave through him. Become what he hated? The thought of it churned his stomach.

His mind flashed back to Kabir: the cruelty in his brother's eyes, the coldness in his voice, the blood on the floor of their home. The memory threatened to consume him, but Siva's voice anchored him back to the present.

Slowly, Ayan let go.

Rahul exhaled sharply, rubbing his arm. He threw a glare but said nothing, recognizing that he had come too close to something he wasn't ready to deal with. The fresher, taking his chance, slipped away into the crowd.

Siva clapped a hand on Ayan's back, giving him a small grin. "See? No broken bones, no unnecessary drama." He tried to keep his tone light, but his eyes held something deeper: relief.

Ayan exhaled, his hands still trembling slightly. He didn't reply, but deep down, he knew that Siva had just saved him from crossing a dangerous line.

That evening, a quiet stillness hung in the air as the city stretched endlessly beyond the terrace, its skyline flickering with neon lights and the occasional honk of distant traffic. The night air was crisp, carrying a faint chill that bit at Ayan's skin as he sat on the ledge, his gaze fixed on the stars above.

He wasn't thinking about anything in particular, at least, that's what he told himself. But thoughts had a way of creeping in when the world quieted down.

Then, out of nowhere, a voice broke the silence.

"Nice view," Siva said casually, stepping onto the terrace with two cans of soft drinks in hand.

Ayan turned, narrowing his eyes. "How the hell do you know where I live?"

Siva grinned, handing him one of the cans. "I know someone... who knows someone... who knows someone... who knows where you live."

Ayan snorted but took the drink anyway. He wasn't sure why. Maybe he was too tired to argue. Maybe he didn't care enough to send Siva away.

Siva plopped down beside him, stretching his legs out and cracking open his can. He took a long sip before leaning back on his elbows, gazing at the sky.

"You ever just look at the stars and wonder if someone else, somewhere far away, is staring at the same ones?" Siva mused. "Makes you feel small, doesn't it?"

Ayan glanced up, taking a sip. "No."

Siva chuckled. "Yeah, figured you'd say that."

They sat in comfortable silence for a while, the hum of the city beneath them blending with the occasional clink of their drinks.

Then, Ayan broke it.

"What did you mean by what you said earlier?"

Siva didn't look at him. "Earlier?"

"About me becoming what I hate."

At that, Siva finally turned his head, studying Ayan for a moment. Then, he sighed, taking another sip of his drink.

"Your past is not that secret, Ayan."

Ayan stiffened slightly, his fingers tightening around the can.

"A lot of people in our college know," Siva continued. "They whisper about it. Wonder about you. But that's not how I knew."

Ayan's eyes flickered toward him. "Then how?"

Siva exhaled slowly. "Years ago, I saw you on TV that day... The Day... you know."

The words sent a cold wave through Ayan's chest.

"That was years ago," Ayan muttered, his voice quieter than he intended.

"Yeah," Siva agreed. "Yeah, you've changed a lot since then. Your height, your hairstyle. But your eyes, Ayan." He took a sip and then met Ayan's gaze. "Your eyes stayed the same."

Ayan held his stare, something unsettling twisting inside him.

Siva leaned back against the ledge. "I can recognize eyes that feel emptiness."

Ayan didn't reply for a long moment. Then, before he could stop himself, the words slipped out.

"Just like your eyes?"

Siva turned his head slightly, as if he hadn't expected that. But instead of denying it, he smirked.

"Somebody did their homework on me."

Siva shrugged, sipping his drink. "It was you, wasn't it? That day at the orphanage. The Father told me one of my 'friends' came by." He glanced at Ayan. "I wasn't sure it was you."

Siva shook his head. "Damn, and here I thought I was being all secretive."

After a brief silence, Siva's fingers traced the rim of his soft drink, his eyes fixed on the horizon. When he finally spoke, his voice was quieter, the usual lightness stripped away.

"My old man was a drunk," he started. "Not the funny kind. The kind that breaks things. And people."

Ayan listened, his grip on the can tightening.

"He used to come home wasted almost every night. Some nights, he'd just pass out. Other nights..." Siva's voice trailed off briefly. "Other nights, my mom and I weren't so lucky."

He let out a short breath, as if steadying himself.

"She always tried to protect me. Whenever he got violent, she'd step in. Take the hits instead." His fingers tapped against the can, a nervous, unconscious habit. "And every single time, she'd look at me and say, 'Siva, go to your room. Don't look back.'"

Siva let out a small chuckle, but there was no humor in it.

"But one night... I did look back."

Ayan's chest tightened.

"I was ten," Siva continued. "We were eating dinner when he came home, already drunk. He started yelling about something: money, his job, I don't even remember. Mom told me to go to my room."

Siva's voice grew quieter.

"And I didn't."

Ayan didn't move, didn't even breathe.

"He hit her," Siva whispered. "Again. And again. And I just stood there. I wanted to do something, but I was a scrawny ten-year-old kid. I was scared. And then, suddenly, she wasn't moving anymore."

The air around them felt heavy, suffocating.

"The police took him away, but it didn't matter," Siva murmured. "She was already gone."

Silence.

Ayan swallowed, his hands clenched around his can.

"He died in police custody a few days later," Siva added. "Some say suicide. Others say the cops beat him to death. I never cared enough to ask."

Another bitter chuckle.

"After that, I ended up in an orphanage. The Father there took care of me. Taught me how to play the guitar. It was the only thing that made me feel something again."

Ayan exhaled through his nose. "That's why you keep running toward people, isn't it?"

Siva looked at him, slightly surprised.

Ayan's voice was quiet, but certain. "Sometimes, you don't talk to everyone because you love the company, you talk to people because you hate being alone."

Siva stared at him for a long moment. Then, he smirked. "Damn, Ayan. You really know how to read people when you want to."

Ayan didn't reply.

Siva leaned back, staring at the sky again. "You know what's funny? No matter how much time passes, I still see her face. Still hear her voice." His fingers tightened around the can. "I don't think that ever goes away."

Ayan looked down at his own hands. He knew what that was like. He saw Kabir's face all the time. Heard his voice in his nightmares.

"The nightmares don't stop," Ayan murmured. "Even when you think you've moved on."

Siva turned his head slightly, looking at him. Then, slowly, he nodded. "Yeah. They don't."

Silence stretched between them again, but this time, it wasn't uncomfortable. It was the kind that understood.

Siva suddenly grinned, breaking the weight of the moment. "Well, that got dark real fast. Damn, Ayan, you really know how to kill the mood."

Ayan rolled his eyes. "You're the one who brought it up, idiot."

Siva chuckled. "Fair point."

They sat there, finishing their drinks in quiet companionship.

EIGHT

NO TAKEBACKS

The annual college festival was something the entire campus looked forward to: colorful decorations, loud music, food stalls, and an energy that made even the most introverted students get involved. Everyone except Ayan.

For him, it was just another day filled with unnecessary noise, a crowd he didn't want to be a part of, and an event he had zero interest in attending. If it were up to him, he'd spend the evening alone in his dorm or at the library. But unfortunately, Siva had other plans.

"You can't hide forever," Siva declared, dramatically flinging an arm around Ayan's shoulder as he dragged him toward the main event area.

"I'm not hiding," Ayan muttered, shaking him off. "I just don't care."

"Wrong answer, my friend." Siva grinned, adjusting his guitar strap. "Today is about fun, and guess what? Fun is mandatory!"

Ayan rolled his eyes. "For you, maybe. I'd rather...

"Yeah, yeah, you'd rather be in a quiet, dark room reading something depressing. I get it. But guess what? That's not happening today."

Ayan sighed, knowing there was no arguing with Siva when he got like this. He looked around, the festival in full swing: students laughing, food stalls filling the air with delicious aromas, and the main stage at the heart of it all, where performances were already underway.

"This entire event is a waste of time," Ayan mumbled.

Siva gasped dramatically. "A waste of time? Ayan, my dear, miserable friend, this is the highlight of the year! People come alive here! Dreams are made, love stories begin, legends are born!"

Ayan shot him a deadpan look. "You just strung together a bunch of dramatic words."

Siva winked. "And yet, I made it sound convincing."

Ayan sighed again, stuffing his hands into his pockets. "Fine. I'll stay for a little while. But I swear, if I hear one more love song from an overly enthusiastic guy with a guitar, I'm leaving."

Siva gasped. "You wound me! I am an overly enthusiastic guy with a guitar!"

Ayan smirked slightly. "Exactly."

They wandered through the crowd, Siva greeting practically everyone while Ayan followed reluctantly. People smiled at Siva, gave him high-fives, and a few even called out his name. Ayan couldn't understand how he had the energy for all this.

"Hey, Siva! You performing tonight?" someone called.

"Wouldn't miss it!" Siva shot back, flashing a grin.

Ayan frowned. "Performing what?"

"Music, obviously. What else?" Siva smirked. "But don't worry, you'll have a role too."

Ayan narrowed his eyes. "I don't like the sound of that."

Siva waved a hand dismissively. "Relax, relax. Just enjoy the festival."

Ayan remained skeptical but decided not to push further. The evening continued with Siva dragging him from one event to another: a food stall where Siva insisted on trying the spiciest challenge, an art gallery where he claimed to be a 'professional critic' despite knowing nothing about painting, and a poetry slam where he loudly whispered terrible rhymes in Ayan's ear, making it impossible for him to keep a straight face.

Despite himself, Ayan found the corners of his lips twitching into a smile more than once.

Then came the talent show.

Siva, being Siva, convinced Ayan to stand near the stage under the pretense of "just watching." What Ayan didn't know was that his so-called friend had a scheme in mind.

As the event began, the host announced the next performer. But instead of the expected name, Siva's voice boomed through the speakers.

"Ladies and gentlemen!"

Ayan's stomach sank.

"Meet my best friend, Ayan! And tonight, he's going to... dance for us!"

For a moment, Ayan thought he had misheard. But then the spotlight landed on him, and the crowd erupted in cheers.

Panic shot through his veins.

He turned to leave, but Siva grabbed his wrist, grinning. "Come on, just one move. For me?"

Ayan's jaw clenched. "I'm going to kill you."

Siva beamed. "Later. But right now, dance."

Ayan shot him a murderous glare, but Siva didn't let go. The crowd cheered louder, clapping and chanting his name. He knew there was no escaping this. If he refused, it would only make things worse.

So, with an exasperated sigh, he took a single step forward, moved his shoulders slightly, and gave the bare minimum of a dance move, just enough to get Siva off his back..

The crowd roared in approval.

Siva doubled over in laughter. "That was terrible!"

"Exactly. Now let me go."

Siva, still laughing, clapped him on the back. "Oh, man. I wish I recorded that."

Ayan huffed, stepping away from the stage and disappearing into the crowd. His face burned with embarrassment, but strangely enough, there was something else, something unexpected..

Adrenaline.

For a brief moment, he had felt… alive.

That night, Ayan hated Siva.

But as much as he hated to admit it, maybe, just maybe, he didn't mind having a friend like him.

NINE

A REASON TO SMILE

Ayan never liked crowded places. He preferred solitude, silence, and the kind of company that didn't require him to talk. Yet, somehow, he found himself standing in front of a mirror, adjusting his shirt, while Siva lounged on his bed, grinning like a fool.

"I can't believe you're actually going to a retirement party," Siva mused, propped up on his elbows. "And voluntarily, too. Who are you, and what have you done with Ayan?"

Ayan shot him a glare through the mirror. "Shut up."

Siva smirked. "No, seriously. If I had known all it took to make you social was an old man retiring, I would've thrown a fake retirement party months ago."

Ayan sighed, running a hand through his hair. "It's not about the party. It's Raghav's night. I owe him that much."

Siva's teasing faded slightly at the sincerity in Ayan's voice. He sat up. "You respect him, don't you?"

Ayan was quiet for a moment before nodding. "More than I ever let on."

Siva tilted his head. "You ever tell him that?"

Ayan exhaled sharply, grabbing his watch from the table. "I don't do 'sentimental,' Siva."

Siva chuckled, shaking his head. "Yeah, yeah, Mr. Tough Guy." Then, his grin returned. "Speaking of sentimental, should I be expecting a heartfelt speech from you tonight? Maybe something along the lines of, 'Raghav, you're like the father I never had'...".

Ayan threw a pillow at his face. "Shut up and get ready."

Siva cackled, dodging the pillow with ease. "I love how you assume I'm coming."

Ayan turned to him with a raised brow. "You're not?"

Siva blinked. Then he grinned. "Well, well, well. Are you inviting me?"

Ayan rolled his eyes. "I just assumed you'd invite yourself like you always do."

Siva clutched his chest dramatically. "I'm touched, truly." He hopped off the bed, grabbing his jacket. "Alright, let's go. Time to charm the old folks."

Ayan sighed but didn't protest. Maybe, just maybe, having Siva around wouldn't be the worst thing.

They took Ayan's bike as he didn't want to sit behind Siva. They arrived just in time, though it seemed Siva's lack of punctuality was starting to rub off on Ayan.

The hall was packed. Officers from different departments, their families, and even some junior trainees had gathered to celebrate Raghav's years of service. The atmosphere was lively, with chatter, laughter, and clinking glasses filling the space.

Ayan walked in with Siva at his side, feeling slightly out of place. He didn't do well in large social settings, but Siva, as always, thrived in them.

"Damn," Siva whistled, looking around. "Your old man is popular."

Ayan hummed in agreement, his eyes scanning the room. It wasn't hard to spot Raghav: he stood near the center, surrounded by a group of officers, including Major Balveer Singh, smiling as they shared old stories.

Ayan hesitated.

Siva nudged him. "Go say hi."

Ayan shot him a look. "I will."

Siva smirked. "What, you need me to hold your hand?"

Ayan glared but said nothing as he approached Raghav.

Raghav turned just as Ayan reached him, his sharp eyes softening slightly. "Ayan."

Ayan gave a small nod. "Congratulations."

Raghav smiled. "You actually came." His gaze shifted to Siva, who was already grinning. "And you brought a friend?"

Siva extended his hand. "Siva Malhotra, sir. Big fan."

Raghav shook his hand, amusement flickering in his eyes. "You must be the infamous Siva I keep hearing about."

Siva gasped. "Hearing about? Ayan, you talk about me?" He turned to Ayan, feigning shock. "I knew you liked me."

Ayan clenched his jaw. "I don't."

Raghav chuckled. It was a strange sight: Ayan, in a social setting, bantering. He had never seen Ayan like this before. He wasn't just existing tonight; he was living.

As the night went on, Ayan found himself surprisingly at ease. Siva had a way of blending into any crowd, and before Ayan knew it, the two of them were sitting at a table, watching the speeches.

Later in the evening, when the crowd had begun to thin, Raghav found himself outside on the balcony, watching the city lights.

"Mind if I join?"

Raghav turned to see Siva stepping outside, holding two glasses of juice. He handed one to Raghav before leaning against the railing.

"You and Ayan seem close," Raghav noted after a moment.

Siva took a sip, nodding. "Yeah. He'd never admit it, but I'm his best friend."

Raghav chuckled. "I believe that."

A beat of silence passed before Raghav spoke again. "You've changed him."

Siva glanced at him. "What do you mean?"

Raghav exhaled, looking back into the hall where Ayan was catching up with Balveer. His posture was relaxed, his expression no longer cold or guarded, but content.

"I've known that boy for years," Raghav murmured. "He doesn't let people in. He's always been distant, keeping everyone at arm's length. But tonight..." He shook his head slightly. "I saw something I haven't seen in a long time."

Siva tilted his head. "And what's that?"

Raghav smiled faintly. "Ayan, smiling."

Siva didn't say anything at first. He simply watched Ayan from a distance, a small grin forming on his lips.

"Yeah, he's a work in progress," Siva admitted. "But he's not as tough as he thinks he is."

Raghav studied him for a moment before nodding. "Thank you, Siva."

Siva turned to him, blinking. "For what?"

"For being there. For showing him that life isn't just about anger and revenge. He needed someone like you."

Siva scoffed. "I didn't do anything special."

"You did more than you think," Raghav said. "You reminded him what it's like to live."

Siva didn't have a response to that. Instead, he just sipped his drink, a rare moment of quiet between them.

After a few minutes, he sighed dramatically. "Alright, this got too deep. I should go annoy Ayan before he gets too comfortable."

Raghav chuckled, watching as Siva made his way back inside. His gaze lingered on Ayan for a moment longer.

Maybe, just maybe, he wouldn't have to worry about Ayan as much anymore.

For the first time in years, Ayan had someone looking out for him. And that, Raghav realized, was more than he could've ever asked for.

TEN
THE DEVIL RETURNS

The evening air was crisp, carrying the lingering echoes of laughter and clinking glasses from the retirement party. Raghav Murthi's career as Commissioner had come to an official close, and the night was meant to be a celebration of his years of service. But for Ayan, the party was just another event to tolerate. The only reason he was even there was out of respect for Raghav. Well... and because of Siva.

"You had fun," Siva teased as they stepped outside into the cool night.

"I tolerated it," Ayan corrected, adjusting his suit.

Siva grinned. "Same thing."

They had planned to leave, but when Ayan went to bid Raghav farewell, another officer informed him that Raghav was in the back garden, engaged in an important call, and had asked not to be disturbed.

"Important call? At his own retirement party?" Ayan muttered, frowning.

The officer shrugged. "You know the Commissioner. Even retirement doesn't stop duty."

Ayan sighed and glanced toward the back garden, a vast open space that stretched toward the edges of the forest. Beyond that, the land sloped into the base of the mountains. It was a quiet, secluded place, perfect for a private conversation..

"Guess we wait," Siva said, stuffing his hands in his pockets.

Ayan nodded, though a strange feeling gnawed at him. He wasn't sure why. Maybe it was instinct, or maybe it was the way the shadows seemed darker than usual under the moonlight.

Siva, being Siva, couldn't stand silence for too long. "So, what do you think Raghav is up to? Secret agent business? Maybe he's planning a final mission before retirement?"

Ayan shot him a flat look. "It's a police case, not a movie."

"Still," Siva leaned against the garden's stone railing, "big-shot officers like him don't take late-night calls unless it's serious. Maybe it's one of those terrorist cases we keep hearing about."

Ayan said nothing, but deep down, he knew Siva was probably right. Raghav had been working on multiple cases related to national security. If this was something urgent enough to interrupt his own farewell party, it had to be big.

Minutes passed. Ayan grew impatient, his gaze drifting toward the shadows between the trees. There was something unsettling about the way the wind rustled through the leaves as if the forest itself was whispering secrets.

Siva shifted beside him, suddenly tense.

Ayan noticed. "What?"

Siva didn't respond immediately. His eyes were locked onto the tree line behind the garden, his normally carefree expression replaced by something unfamiliar: unease.

"I don't know," Siva muttered. "I thought I saw something... or someone."

Ayan's gaze followed his, scanning the darkness. "You're imagining things."

"Maybe." Siva exhaled. "Maybe not."

Ayan wanted to dismiss it, but something about the way Siva said it made his stomach twist. He'd learned to trust his instincts over the years, and Siva, despite his constant idiocy, had good instincts.

Finally, after what felt like an eternity, Raghav emerged from the shadows, his face tensed. He walked toward them with an air of seriousness, but there was also something else...something mysterious.

"What was that about?" Ayan asked.

Raghav studied him for a moment before sighing. "We got intel. A breakthrough on a terrorist operation we've been tracking for months."

Ayan's brows furrowed. "How serious?"

"Serious enough that I almost walked out of my own retirement party," Raghav said with a small smirk. Then, his expression hardened. "They're planning something big. My team is moving in soon."

There was a quiet weight to his words. Even Siva, usually the first to crack a joke, stayed silent.

Ayan felt a strange sense of admiration. Even after stepping down, Raghav was still in the fight, still doing what he believed in. "Your team has been doing a damn good job," he said finally.

Raghav glanced at him, and a small, rare smile crossed his face. He placed a firm hand on Ayan's shoulder. "Thank you."

It wasn't just about the case. Ayan knew that. It was about everything. The way Raghav had taken him in, raised him, and given him a life when he had nothing.

"Good night, Raghav," Ayan said.

Raghav nodded. "Good night, Ayan."

And with that, Ayan and Siva left the party, stepping into the cold night.

The night air rushed past them, cool and sharp, as Ayan and Siva sped down the deserted road on Ayan's bike. The party had been unexpectedly pleasant, and Ayan had actually enjoyed himself, something he never thought possible.

Siva, seated behind Ayan, stretched his arms dramatically. "Man, I gotta say, you in a suit was a sight to behold. You almost looked human."

Ayan didn't respond. His mind was elsewhere.

"You know," Siva continued, his voice carrying over the roar of the engine, "I think Raghav was actually happy to see you smile. The man looked like he was gonna cry tears of joy."

Ayan sighed. "You talk too much."

"Someone's grumpy. You need some alcohol in your system," Siva chuckled. "Or maybe just more parties."

Ayan ignored him, focusing on the road ahead. The streets were empty, dimly lit by streetlights casting long shadows across the pavement. The road stretched through the outskirts of the city, flanked by trees on either side.

Then, Ayan felt it.

A shift in the air.

A cold sensation was crawling up his spine.

Siva must have sensed something too, because he stopped talking. His grip on Ayan's shoulder tightened slightly.

The bike's headlight cut through the darkness as they turned a sharp bend.

And then they saw him.

A lone figure stood in the middle of the road, directly in their path.

Tall. Broad. Unmoving.

Ayan's breath hitched. Even before the light fully illuminated him, he knew who it was.

Kabir.

Ayan barely had time to react before his instincts kicked in. He yanked the brake hard, the tires screeching against the asphalt. The bike skidded violently, but Ayan controlled it, stopping just a few feet away from the man who had haunted his nightmares for years.

Siva cursed, nearly falling off. "What the hell, man? You trying to kill us?"

But Ayan wasn't listening. His hands clenched around the handlebars as he glared at the man standing before them.

Kabir stepped forward, the headlight casting his face in sharp relief. His eyes, dark and unreadable, met Ayan's.

"Hello Brother,"

Kabir said with his lips curled into a smirk."I missed you. Did you miss me?"

Rage boiled inside Ayan. He didn't think. He didn't hesitate.

He lunged.

Jumping off the bike, he swung a punch straight at Kabir's face.

Kabir didn't move until the last second. Effortlessly, he tilted his head, the punch missing him by mere inches. Ayan followed up with another strike, this time a feint, using his left hand to throw a quick jab before aiming a kick at Kabir's ribs."

It was fast. Fueled with rage. Years of training compressed into every movement.

And yet...

Kabir blocked it all.

Effortlessly.

He moved like a shadow, fluid and unreadable, parrying every strike with practiced ease. Ayan gritted his teeth, pushing harder, faster. He twisted, delivering a spinning kick meant to take Kabir off balance.

Kabir caught his leg mid-air.

Before Ayan could react, a fist slammed into his stomach.

Pain exploded through his core.

Kabir didn't hold back.

Ayan gasped as the impact knocked the wind out of him. He staggered, but sheer determination forced him to stay upright. He had barely regained his footing when Kabir struck again.

A brutal knee to the ribs.

Ayan coughed, tasting blood. He barely had time to register the pain before Kabir's fist crashed into his jaw, sending him sprawling to the ground.

Siva yelled and jumped in, attempting to tackle Kabir. It was a foolish move.

Kabir barely glanced at him before grabbing Siva by the collar and tossing him aside like a ragdoll. Siva hit the pavement hard, groaning in pain.

Ayan struggled to stand. His vision blurred, but he forced his body to move. He couldn't lose. Not to him.

Kabir tilted his head slightly, with a calm voice. "You've trained," he noted. "But you're still too weak."

Ayan growled, charging at him again. He threw a flurry of punches, using everything he had, but Kabir dodged each one effortlessly. Then, with a swift counter, he struck Ayan's ribs again.

The impact was like a sledgehammer.

Ayan dropped to one knee, panting heavily. He could barely stand.

Siva, despite knowing he stood no chance, got back up.

Kabir raised an eyebrow. "You again?"

Siva wiped the blood from his lip. "Yeah. Me again."

Kabir moved so fast that Ayan barely saw it. One second, Siva was standing; the next, he was slammed against a nearby lamppost, his back hitting the cold metal with a sickening thud.

Kabir held him there, his hand gripping Siva's throat, not too tight, but firm enough to make a point. "Why don't you run?" Kabir asked, his voice almost amused. "Who is he to you?"

Siva coughed but didn't look away. His eyes burned with defiance. "He's my best friend," Siva said, looking at Ayan before turning back to Kabir.

His eyes locked onto Kabir's. "I'm more of a brother to him than you ever were."

For the first time, Kabir paused. Then, slowly, he smirked.

"Interesting," he murmured.

He released Siva, letting him drop to the ground.

Ayan, still struggling to get up, clenched his fists. "Bastard..."

Kabir turned his gaze back to Ayan. His smirk faded slightly, replaced by something colder. "I don't have time for you two." He glanced at the distant city lights. "I have some fireworks to burn."

Ayan's eyes widened. "What?"

Kabir didn't answer. He turned, walking away, his figure slowly fading into the darkness of the trees.

Ayan pushed himself up. "Kabir!" he shouted, trying to move, but his body betrayed him. He collapsed to his knees, gasping for breath.

Siva groaned, rolling onto his back. "Damn... your brother's a monster."

Ayan barely heard him. His heart pounded against his ribs, his breathing ragged.

He had waited years for this moment. Trained for it. Dreamed of the day he would finally face Kabir.

And he had failed.

Kabir was still untouchable. Still stronger, faster. Still, the same nightmare Ayan could never escape.

But as the echoes of Kabir's footsteps disappeared into the night, one thing became clear.

This wasn't over. Not even close.

ELEVEN

THE CRUMBLING CASTLE

Ayan slowly opened his eyes.

The sun was too bright.

For a moment, everything was blurry: just light and warmth and the distant sound of waves. Then, the world settled into focus. The salty breeze tickled his face, carrying the rhythmic sound of the ocean crashing against the shore. The cries of seagulls echoed in the air, circling above him.

He looked down at his tiny hands.

Small. Soft.

Something felt... strange.

Then, a voice called out to him.

"Ayan, come! It's almost done!"

He turned toward the sound.

Kabir.

But... he looked younger.

Ayan blinked.

His brother wasn't the tall, intimidating figure he had become in Ayan's memories. He wasn't the monster that haunted his nightmares.

He was just a thirteen-year-old boy, kneeling in the sand, carefully building a grand castle.

Ayan hesitated, confusion creeping in. Something wasn't right.

But then, Kabir looked up at him.

And he smiled.

That warm, familiar smile Ayan used to love.

All the uncertainty melted away.

Ayan grinned, running toward him. "Coming, bhaiya!"

Kabir chuckled as Ayan plopped down beside him, breathless with excitement.

"It's missing something," Kabir said, tilting his head as he looked at the sandcastle he was making. "We need decorations."

Ayan's eyes widened. "Shells!"

"Exactly."

"I'll get them!"

Before Kabir could say anything else, Ayan was already up, dashing toward the water. His small feet sank into the wet sand with each step. The waves brushed against his ankles, cool and refreshing.

He crouched, scanning the shore.

One by one, he picked the prettiest shells: white, pink, and speckled brown, clutching them tightly in his tiny hands.

Behind him, Kabir watched.

Ayan knew.

Even though Kabir wasn't saying anything, he was always keeping an eye on him. Always making sure he didn't go too far.

Ayan smiled to himself.

His hands were full now. He turned back, ran back to Kabir with excitement bubbling in his chest.

"I got...

His foot caught on something.

His body pitched forward.

And in a split second, he crashed straight into the sandcastle.

The fortress crumbled instantly.

Ayan gasped. His hands flew to the sand, trying to fix what was already ruined, but the damage was done. The castle was nothing but a heap of broken walls.

Tears stung his eyes. He lifted his head slowly, guilt twisting in his small chest.

He expected anger.

But Kabir was already kneeling beside him.

His hands were on Ayan's shoulders, checking, searching.

"Are you hurt?" Kabir's voice was calm, steady.

Ayan blinked at him. "B-but... your castle..."

Kabir ruffled his hair, his warm smile never fading. "Stupid brother," he said, shaking his head. "I don't care about the castle. I only care about you."

Ayan's heart swelled..

Then...

A voice called from behind.

"Ayan! It's time for dinner."

Ayan blinked.

The beach disappeared.

Now, he was at home.

The dining table was set, the warm glow of the overhead lights making everything feel cozy and familiar. His father sat at the head of the table, and his mother placed food onto the plates.

Ayan scrambled into his chair, stomach rumbling.

Kabir sat beside him, just like always.

His mother smiled as she set a plate in front of him.

"What's for dinner, Ammi?" Ayan asked eagerly.

"Palak paneer, chana masala and roti"

Ayan's nose scrunched. "Eww. I don't want it."

His father sighed. "Ayan, we've been eating chicken for the past week. Let's have something different today."

"No! I want chicken," Ayan insisted.

"There's no more chicken, beta," his mother said gently. "I'll make some tomorrow, I promise."

But Ayan crossed his arms stubbornly. "No! I don't want to eat this."

His father's voice hardened. "Either eat what's on your plate, or you'll have no food for a week."

Frustration bubbled in Ayan's chest. He pushed the plate away. It clattered loudly against the table.

Jumping down from the chair, he stormed off to the couch, arms still crossed.

His vision blurred slightly from tears.

The room was silent.

Then, Kabir stood.

"Excuse me Abba, I'll eat later," he said.

His father frowned. "Why?"

Kabir shrugged. "I think I left the computer on."

And just like that, he walked upstairs.

Minutes passed.

Ayan's father finished eating, wiping his hands with a towel. "How long does it take to turn off a computer?"

His mother smiled, as if she knew something. "Maybe he remembered some work."

His father grumbled, then headed to his room.

The moment his door clicked shut, Kabir returned.

His hair was messy, damp with sweat.

His mother noticed instantly. "What happened to you?"

Kabir waved her off. "Nothing, Ammi. Never mind."

Then, he knelt in front of Ayan.

His voice was soft. "Do you want chicken?"

Ayan's eyes widened. "Yes..."

Kabir grinned and pulled out a small paper bag. "Here you go."

Ayan's heart soared.

He took the bag eagerly, feeling the warmth of the food inside. He didn't ask how Kabir got it. He already knew.

Kabir snuck out.

Climbed through his window. Down the tree.

Ran through the dark streets.

Just for him.

They sat at the table again, side by side. Ayan took a bite, happy, safe.

Then...

Something changed.

Kabir was still beside him.

Still smiling.

But something was... wrong.

His smile didn't fade.

It stretched.

Slowly.

Too wide.

The warmth in his eyes flickered, like a candle struggling to stay lit.

Ayan's chest tightened.

He blinked.

The lights above began to dim.

The room shifted.

The walls...

They were no longer white.

They were turning red.

A drop of something splashed onto the table.

Ayan froze.

Another drop.

Then another.

He looked down.

His hands, covered in blood.

His plate, soaked in red.

A wet, choked sound came from beside him.

Ayan turned his head.

His father was slumped in his chair, blood oozing from his throat.

His mother was on the floor, mouth open in a silent scream, eyes frozen in horror.

His breath came in short gasps. "No... no, no, no..."

Kabir moved.

Ayan looked at him.

His stomach dropped.

Kabir's face was splattered with blood.

He was still smiling.

He stood up, slow and deliberate, picking up a knife from the table.

Ayan's heart pounded.

The walls around him were shifting, pulsing like living flesh. The floor was soaked in blood.

Kabir took a step toward him.

Ayan stumbled backward.

His back hit the wall.

No escape.

Kabir tilted his head, gripping the knife tightly.

"I only care about you," he whispered.

The words were wrong. Twisted.

His voice was too soft, too gentle, like a lullaby sung by something inhuman.

The knife rose.

His voice dropped to a whisper.

"Die, little brother."

Ayan screamed...

And then,

He woke up.

His chest heaved violently, his body drenched in sweat.

The world spun around him.

His hands were shaking.

He didn't know what was real.

He could still hear the blood dripping. He could still see the knife.

A voice cut through the haze.

"Ayan."

It was steady. Strong.

He turned his head.

Raghav stood beside his hospital bed.

"You're safe, Ayan, I am here".

Ayan's fingers curled into fists. His breath, ragged and uneven, began to slow. Reality settled in, bit by bit, pushing away the lingering nightmare.

His throat felt dry, but he forced himself to speak. His voice, though steady, held the faintest trace of fear.

"Where is Siva?"

A voice came from the right corner of the room, light but reassuring.

"Right here, pal."

Ayan turned his head. Siva was sitting on his own hospital bed, leaning against the wall with his legs stretched out in front of him. He looked fine, at least, compared to Ayan. He had a broken wrist and a few bruises on his face, but nothing that seemed too serious. His usual grin wasn't there, but his presence was enough to ease the tight knot in Ayan's chest.

Siva had witnessed the way Ayan thrashed in his sleep, mumbling incoherent words, gripping the sheets as if he were fighting something unseen. He had never seen Ayan like that before. He had always known Ayan was closed off, haunted by something he refused to talk about, but now, he understood just how deeply he was fighting with his past.

And in that moment, Siva realized something.
Ayan wasn't just haunted by the past.

He was still living in it.

Siva remained silent, not because he had nothing to say, but because, for once, he understood that words wouldn't help. Jokes wouldn't fix this. Teasing wouldn't pull Ayan out of it. This was deeper than he had imagined. A wound that time hadn't healed.

And that realization unsettled him.

Ayan, on the other hand, had it worse. A few broken ribs, cuts along his arms, and a deep gash on his forehead. The memory of the fight came back in flashes: Kabir's unreadable smirk, the force of his blows, the way he overpowered Ayan without breaking a sweat.

For a brief moment, relief washed over Ayan at the sight of Siva still alive. But as quickly as it came, it was replaced by a burning anger. His fingers clenched into the blanket, and with great effort, he tried to push himself up. A sharp pain shot through his ribs, making him wince.

"Don't even try it," Raghav warned, placing a firm hand on his shoulder. "You'll need to stay in bed for a few weeks."

Ayan gritted his teeth, his jaw tightening. His anger was barely contained, simmering beneath the surface.

"It was him," he muttered, his voice filled with frustration. "Kabir."

The room fell into silence. A heaviness settled between them, the weight of that name pressing down like a storm cloud.

After a long pause, Raghav finally spoke, his voice measured and firm.

"I know. And I think I know why he was here."

Ayan's eyes snapped to Raghav, surprise flickering through his frustration. Even Siva, who had been mostly quiet, perked up with curiosity.

"Why?" Ayan demanded.

Raghav exhaled, rubbing his temples as though the explanation itself was exhausting.

"The intel we received at the party," he began, "was about a terrorist activity in Andheri. They were planning to detonate a bomb in one of the malls there. We intercepted the information just in time, and with the bomb squad and our special forces, we were able to catch them in the act while they were planting it."

Ayan listened, his heart pounding, but Raghav wasn't done.

"There were three men caught. But the information we had said there were four. We didn't know where the last one was."

Ayan's stomach sank. He already knew what was coming.

"Now we do."

Siva let out a slow breath, his usual carefree demeanor nowhere to be found. His expression was unreadable, but Ayan could tell that even he was shaken by this revelation.

"Kabir," Ayan whispered. His hands gripped the sheets, his frustration reaching its peak.

"Yes," Raghav confirmed. "While we were out there stopping them, Kabir was here. With you."

Siva was speechless, and for once, he didn't try to crack a joke to lighten the mood. This wasn't something he could joke about.

Ayan's head swirled with thoughts.

His mind couldn't process it all at once. He clenched his jaw so hard it ached.

"All these years," he muttered under his breath, "All these years I trained. I pushed myself beyond my limits, and still..." His fingers dug into the blanket as his frustration boiled over. "Still, I was no match for him."

He felt helpless. Weak. No matter how hard he fought, he couldn't even land a proper hit on Kabir. The years of training, the pain he endured, the discipline...It all felt meaningless.

Raghav, sensing the storm brewing inside Ayan, placed a reassuring hand on his shoulder.

"There is a right moment for everything, Ayan," he said firmly. "This wasn't the time."

Ayan turned to look at him, eyes burning with frustration.

"It wasn't about skill," Raghav continued. "It was about being ruthless."

The words hit Ayan like a punch to the gut. He wanted to argue, wanted to insist that he should have been strong enough, but deep down, he knew Raghav was right.

Kabir didn't just fight to win. He fought to break his opponents.

And Ayan wasn't like that.

"Being strong isn't just about how well you fight," Raghav went on. "It's about knowing when to fight and when to step back. And right now, you need to heal."

Ayan clenched his fists. He didn't want to step back. He wanted to face Kabir. He wanted to end this.

But right now, he couldn't.

Siva, who had been listening quietly, finally spoke.

"Well," he sighed, cracking a small grin despite the tension. "That was a hell of a night, huh?"

Ayan shot him a look, but Siva just shrugged.

"Come on, Ayan," he said, stretching his injured arm. "We survived getting our asses kicked by a psychopath. That's gotta count for something, right?"

Ayan didn't answer.

"Hey," Siva nudged his foot against Ayan's. "For what it's worth, you held your ground. Even when you knew you couldn't win."

Ayan stayed silent for a moment before finally sighing. "Yeah. That's not really comforting."

Siva grinned. "Didn't think it would be."

Raghav looked at Ayan and Siva, his expression calm but firm.

"I need to get back to the station and give a proper briefing," he said. "Even though I'm no longer on the force, last night's details need to be shared with the new commissioner."

He turned toward the door, then glanced back at them.

"You boys, get some rest. I'll be back in the evening."

Then, with a smirk, he added, "Oh, and by the way... your friends are here."

As soon as Raghav left, the door creaked open again. The room, previously filled with tense silence, was now invaded by the voices of excited visitors. Ayan barely reacted, still caught up in his thoughts, but Siva immediately looked toward the entrance.

Arun, Meenakshi, Imtiaz, and Anushka entered, carrying bags of fruits and flowers. They were some of Siva's closest friends in college: loud, chaotic, and full of energy. Out of all his friendships, Ayan was the one Siva valued the most, but these four had become an integral part of his life, always surrounding him with their endless banter and drama.

The second they stepped inside, Arun wasted no time.

"Oh wow, Siva. I didn't know you were this desperate to bunk classes," he teased, smirking. "A broken wrist? A few bruises? That's the best excuse you could come up with?"

Siva rolled his eyes. "Yeah, yeah, laugh it up. Next time, I'll make sure to get hit by a truck for extra sympathy points."

Imtiaz, meanwhile, had already made himself comfortable. He walked over to Siva's bed, nudged him to move aside, and sat down with zero hesitation. Then, as if it were his own house, he reached for the fruit basket they had brought. Without shame, he plucked a grape and popped it into his mouth.

Siva narrowed his eyes. "I thought that was for me."

Imtiaz, still chewing, shrugged. "Fruits are for patients, not for guys who get admitted to hospitals just to flirt with cute nurses."

A snort of laughter came from Arun, while Meenakshi smacked Imtiaz's arm. "Shh! Stop it, yaar! He already had a rough day," she scolded.

"Exactly," Siva added with a dramatic sigh. "Show some respect for the injured."

The room was lively. Everyone was engaged, throwing jokes and comments around like a tennis match, everyone except one.

Anushka.

She hadn't spoken a word since stepping inside. She was standing a little away from the group, her hands nervously gripping the handles of her purse. She had always been the quietest of them, but today, she seemed different. Her head was down, her face looked pale, and her usually warm hazel eyes were dull with worry.

Her eyes reflected something deeper, an unspoken pain that only she knew.

Anushka was a beautiful young lady: beautiful enough to make a man fall in love. But it wasn't just her looks; it was something in the way she carried herself, the quiet elegance that never felt forced. She had hazel eyes that held a depth, a softness that made people feel at ease in her presence. Her pale skin had a natural glow, and her dark hair, with soft curls framing her face, added to her understated charm.

Anushka was the only daughter of one of Mumbai's richest businessmen, but wealth never defined her. She was humble, down-to-earth, and genuinely kind. And, unknown to Siva, she cared about him deeply.

Meenakshi, Arun, and Imtiaz knew about Anushka's feelings for Siva. They had seen it long ago: the way her gaze softened when she looked at Siva, the way she was always the first to notice when something was wrong with him.

But Siva never noticed. Or maybe... he did, and he chose to ignore it.

Anushka took a small step forward, finally gathering the courage to speak.

"...Are you okay?" Her voice was soft, careful, as if afraid that her words would break him. "Does it... hurt?"

The room fell silent for a moment.

Meenakshi and Arun exchanged a look, understanding what Anushka was really asking. It wasn't just about his injuries: it was about last night, about whatever had happened that left both Siva and Ayan in this condition.

Siva, of course, responded in his usual way.

"Aah, this?" He motioned to his broken wrist and bruised face, leaning back casually. "Just a scratch. I'll be back on track by tomorrow."

A small smile finally appeared on Anushka's face.

She pulled a chair and sat near him, resting her hands in her lap. Siva didn't notice, but Meenakshi did. Arun did. They knew she wasn't there just because Siva was injured: she was there because she had spent the whole night worrying about him.

Meanwhile, Arun and Meenakshi grabbed some apples and oranges from the fruit basket and walked toward Ayan.

Ayan, who had been completely silent the entire time.

Unlike Siva, he wasn't part of this group. He never spoke to them, never acknowledged their presence. But they didn't want to treat him any differently just because of that.

Meenakshi held out the fruit. "These are some apples and oranges. We bought extra for you, too."

For the first time, Ayan looked up.

"...Thank you."

That was the first response they had ever gotten from him.

It wasn't much, just two words. But to Meenakshi and Arun, it felt like a small victory.

A few feet away, Imtiaz finally decided to ask the question that had been burning in everyone's mind.

"So... what happened to you guys?" He looked at Siva. "Fell off the bike?"

Siva smirked. "Oh well, nothing like that. We just got a visit from his big brother. Nice fellow, not much of a talker, though."

The room went completely silent.

Anushka's grip on her purse tightened, and her eyes widened.

Meenakshi, Arun, and Imtiaz froze, exchanging uneasy glances; they all knew about Ayan's past, about what his brother had done. But hearing Siva say it so casually sent a chill through them.

Anushka was the first to react.

"Kabir..." she whispered.

The name had barely left her lips before she realized what she had done. Her eyes widened, and she quickly looked at Ayan, guilt flashing across her face. "I'm sorry..."

Siva, sensing the tension, quickly tried to lighten the mood. "It's fine. He's gone now. Ayan gave some good punches back, too."

Arun raised an eyebrow. "And you?"

Siva smirked dramatically. "Oh, me? I was like fire. He couldn't even touch me. You could say he ran away because of me."

Meenakshi rolled her eyes. "Oh really? You? Fought Kabir Yusuf Ali? And he ran away because of you?"

"Exactly." Siva nodded. "It was glorious."

She scoffed. "You scoring 100% on a math test is more believable than that."

A small laugh broke out.

It was brief, but it was enough to bring some normalcy back into the room.

Except for Ayan.

He hadn't reacted to any of it.

He was still staring at the wall, his expression blank, his hands resting on his lap. Maybe he had just zoned out. Or maybe... he was reliving last night. Maybe he was already planning his next move.

No one asked.

They knew Ayan well enough to understand that his silence was never empty; it was always filled with something darker, something heavier.

But for now, they let him be.

For now, they let the air remain light, let the tension dissolve into playful bickering.

Siva got discharged the next day, but instead of going home, he decided to stay beside Ayan.

He didn't like the idea of Ayan waking up alone in a hospital room.

He missed a few classes, but that wasn't a big deal. Whenever he needed a change of clothes, he'd run home quickly and come right back. Most of his time was spent sitting beside Ayan, scrolling through his phone, chatting with the nurses, or dozing off in the uncomfortable hospital chair.

Two weeks passed.

Ayan finally got discharged.

The morning was crisp, the sky painted in soft shades of orange and pink as Ayan stepped out of the hospital doors. The outside world felt oddly unfamiliar after weeks of sterile white walls and beeping monitors. He exhaled, relishing the fresh air, but even that small movement sent a dull ache through his ribs. His injuries weren't fully healed, but he was past the point of caring.

Siva was the one who drove him home, refusing to let him take a cab.

The bike ride was quieter than usual. Siva tried filling the silence with random humming, but Ayan wasn't in the mood for chatter. His mind was still stuck on that night.

The streets passed in a blur until they finally pulled up to Ayan's room. Ayan pushed himself off the bike, wincing slightly, and made his way to his room. But as soon as he stepped inside, something felt off. His sharp eyes scanned the space, instantly noticing something that hadn't been there before.

A guitar, a few bags.

A pillow and blanket were folded neatly on the bed in the extra room.

Ayan frowned. Whose stuff is this?

He turned toward Siva, who was leaning casually against the doorframe, looking entirely too comfortable.

"Those are yours," Ayan said, his voice flat. "Why are they here?"

Siva grinned, as if he had been waiting for this moment. "Because I decided to let myself live here."

Ayan's expression darkened. "You what?"

Siva stepped inside, stretching his arms like he already owned the place. "Listen, you already have two rooms, and you're not even using the other one. It's just collecting dust. So, I'm taking it."

Ayan crossed his arms, ignoring the pain in his ribs. "That's not how this works."

"I'll pay half the rent."

"It's not about money...

"And," Siva cut him off, "you need help. You can barely walk straight."

Ayan scowled. "I don't need help." He turned toward his room, intent on proving his point.

But the moment he took a step, his balance faltered. His vision blurred slightly from exhaustion and pain. His ribs screamed in protest. Before he could steady himself, he felt a firm grip on his arm, stopping his fall.

"Yeah, you clearly don't need any help," Siva smirked, holding Ayan up effortlessly.

Ayan clenched his jaw in frustration. He hated this. Hated feeling weak. Hated the fact that Siva was right.

Siva helped him onto the bed, making sure he was comfortable before stepping back.

Ayan exhaled sharply, defeated. He knew Siva well enough by now. There was no getting rid of him once he had made up his mind.

Still, Ayan glared at him. "Fine. But don't touch my stuff."

Siva gave a mock salute. "Aye, aye, Captain."

Ayan leaned back against the pillows, closing his eyes for a moment. His body ached, exhaustion pulling at him, but his mind refused to rest. There was another reason why he didn't argue harder.

Because Kabir had seen Siva.

And that meant Siva's life might be in danger.

Keeping him close was the only way to make sure he didn't become another casualty.

Whether Siva realized it or not, he had just stepped deeper into Ayan's world. A world full of ghosts, blood, and shadows that never truly left.

The next morning, for the first time in two weeks, Siva decided to return to college. Not just to pick up his study materials for the upcoming exams, but also to see his friends, grab a coffee, and talk about everything that had happened. He needed a break, even if it was just for a few hours.

Walking through the bustling college corridors, Siva felt like he had stepped into another world. It was almost jarring how normal everything was. Students hurried to their lectures, some chatting in groups, others sitting in corners, noses buried in books. Life had moved on as if nothing had happened.

As soon as he reached the campus café, he spotted his gang sitting at their usual table. They had already ordered, and a steaming cup of coffee was waiting for him.

"Look who finally decided to show up," Arun smirked, leaning back in his chair.

Siva rolled his eyes and sat down. "Yeah, yeah. I was a little busy, you know, making sure our friend didn't die."

Imtiaz shook his head. "Man, it's weird not having you around. College felt... quieter."

Arun chuckled. "Yeah, no one was around to annoy the professors or flirt with the seniors."

Siva grinned but didn't respond. His thoughts were elsewhere.

Anushka, who had been silent so far, finally spoke. "How's Ayan?"

Siva hesitated for a moment before answering. "Physically, he's recovering. But mentally..." He sighed, running a hand through his hair. "I don't know. He's shutting everyone out. It's like he's trying to push away anything that reminds him of the past, but at the same time, he can't escape it."

There was a moment of silence as everyone processed his words.

Imtiaz finally asked the question that had been lingering in everyone's mind.

"Why are you doing this much for him, Siva?" He leaned forward, resting his elbows on the table. "We all know you're a good guy, but don't you think it's a bit too much? You almost got killed a few weeks ago, and he's not even that welcoming towards you."

Arun and Meenakshi exchanged glances. Anushka, who had been stirring her coffee absentmindedly, finally looked up. No one wanted to be the first to say it, but now that Imtiaz had, they all waited for Siva's response.

Siva smirked, shaking his head. "You guys wouldn't get it even if I told you."

Imtiaz scoffed. "Try me."

Siva smirked at first, shaking his head as if trying to brush it off, but then he sighed, his expression turning serious.

"I know his pain," he said, his voice quieter than before. "I see his darkness, I see his loss." His fingers traced the rim of his coffee cup absentmindedly. "And somehow, I feel connected to him. I don't know why, but I do."

The table fell silent.

"I guess..." Siva continued, looking off into the distance. "I feel kinda sad seeing him like this. He is like a brother I never had. Feels like family."

Anushka's gaze softened, and Meenakshi exhaled, resting her chin on her hand. Arun shifted uncomfortably in his chair, not quite sure how to respond. Imtiaz, who had expected some kind of joke or half-hearted answer, found himself caught off guard.

After a moment, he cleared his throat and muttered, "Damn, man. Didn't know you felt that way."

Siva grinned, trying to lighten the mood. "Well, I'm full of surprises."

The conversation drifted back to something else, but that moment lingered in everyone's minds. They realized Siva wasn't just being stubborn; he genuinely cared about Ayan. And no matter how much Ayan tried to push him away, Siva wasn't going anywhere.

They talked for a while longer, sipping coffee and discussing everything from upcoming exams to the latest college gossip. For the first time in weeks, Siva felt like things were normal again. But deep down, he knew that normal wasn't something Ayan had anymore.

After an hour or so, he glanced at his watch and sighed. "Alright, I should get back. If I leave Ayan alone for too long, who knows what kind of trouble he'll get into."

By the time he reached home, the sun had begun its descent, casting a warm orange glow across the city. The house was quiet when he stepped inside, and for a moment, he thought Ayan might be resting.

But then he saw him.

Ayan was lying on the floor, motionless.

For a split second, panic seized Siva's chest. He rushed forward, kneeling beside him. "Ayan! Hey, wake up!"

Ayan's face was pale, his body covered in a thin layer of sweat. His breathing was uneven, but at least he was breathing. Siva quickly checked for injuries, but nothing seemed out of the ordinary until he noticed the position of his arms.

Push-ups.

Siva let out a slow breath, realization dawning on him. Ayan had been pushing himself too hard again.

He gently shook Ayan's shoulder. "Come on, man, wake up."

Ayan stirred slightly, his eyelids fluttering open. He groaned, clearly disoriented. "What...?"

Siva let out a relieved sigh. "You passed out, dumbass. What the hell were you thinking?"

Ayan blinked, his eyes still unfocused. "Nothing, I am fine..."

Siva scoffed. "Yeah, well, I can see that. What's wrong with you? You just got out of the hospital, and you're already trying to break yourself again?"

Ayan tried to sit up, but his body protested. He winced, his hand instinctively going to his ribs.

Siva shook his head. "You're unbelievable."

Ayan exhaled slowly, his frustration evident. "I have to get stronger."

Siva's expression softened. He sat down on the floor beside Ayan. "You're not weak. But you're also not invincible. You have to give yourself time to recover."

Ayan didn't respond. He just stared at the ceiling, lost in thought.

Siva nudged him. "Come on, let's get you off the floor. If Raghav sees this, He will kill both of us."

With some effort, he helped Ayan up and onto the bed. Ayan was reluctant, but he was too exhausted to argue.

Siva sat beside him. "Listen, I know you want to be stronger. I get it. But you can't do it like this. Killing yourself in the process isn't a strength, Ayan. It's stupidity."

Ayan finally looked at him. "You wouldn't understand."

Siva held his gaze. "Maybe not. But I'm still here."

Ayan didn't respond, but he knew Siva was right; there was no defeating Kabir if he didn't live long enough to try.

TWELVE

BETWEEN RAINDROPS

The next afternoon, the gang met at their usual spot on campus. The courtyard was buzzing with students, some rushing to their classes, others lounging around, enjoying the cloudy weather. Siva leaned back on the bench, stretching his arms as he exhaled loudly.

"I need to get some printouts from the other block," he announced. "Anyone coming?"

Imtiaz and Meenakshi exchanged glances before shaking their heads. "We're heading to the library," Imtiaz said. "Got a project to finish."

"Figures," Siva muttered. "Where is Arun?" He turned, "Is he not coming today?"

"He said he won't be coming today," Meenakshi replied.

Siva sighed and was about to leave when Anushka spoke up. "I'll come."

He turned to her, raising an eyebrow. "You sure? It's just printouts. Not exactly an exciting adventure."

Anushka shrugged. "I have nothing better to do."

"Fair enough," Siva said, getting up.

The two of them walked toward the other block, the air between them calm but quiet. Anushka wasn't the type to fill silences with meaningless chatter, and Siva didn't mind. He preferred easy conversations, ones that didn't require effort.

"You seem distracted lately," Anushka said after a while.

Siva glanced at her. "Do I?"

"Yeah. You're usually... I don't know, more talkative. Lighter."

Siva smirked. "Are you saying I've lost my charm?"

Anushka rolled her eyes. "I'm saying you've been different. Since... you know, everything happened."

Siva didn't answer immediately. It was true. A lot had changed in the past few weeks, but he didn't know how to explain it. He wasn't used to thinking too deeply about things, let alone talking about them.

"I guess," he finally said. "I mean, things have been... intense."

Anushka nodded, understanding. "Yeah."

They reached the print shop, where Siva handed over his USB drive. The small room smelled of fresh ink, and the hum of printers filled the silence.

Anushka crossed her arms, leaning against the counter. "You ever think about taking a break?"

Siva raised an eyebrow. "A break from what?"

"From... all of this. Taking care of Ayan. Worrying about things you don't usually worry about."

Siva chuckled. "That's the thing about caring: you don't get to take breaks."

Anushka tilted her head slightly, watching him. There was something about the way he said it: lighthearted, yet strangely sincere.

Before she could say anything else, the worker handed Siva his printouts, and they stepped back outside.

The sky had darkened, heavy clouds rolling in as the first few raindrops fell onto the pavement.

"Uh-oh," Siva muttered, looking up.

Anushka did the same, just as the drizzle turned into a full-blown shower. Within seconds, students were scrambling for cover, laughter and hurried footsteps echoing around them.

"Of course," Anushka sighed, pulling out her umbrella. With a practiced motion, she flicked it open. "Come on," she said, stepping closer.

Siva hesitated for a second before stepping under, their shoulders nearly touching. "Well, this is cozy," he teased.

"Just be grateful I had an umbrella," Anushka shot back.

The rain, instead of slowing down, only intensified. It poured heavily, drenching everything in sight.

"We should wait this out," Anushka suggested, nodding toward a small covered area near a tree.

Siva nodded, and they ran toward it, water splashing under their shoes. Once under the shelter, Anushka shook off her umbrella, while Siva ran a hand through his damp hair.

"That escalated quickly," he muttered.

Anushka smiled. "Yeah. Mumbai rains are unpredictable."

For a moment, there was silence. The rain drummed against the roof, a steady rhythm that filled the space between them.

Siva leaned against the pillar, his gaze drifting toward Anushka. He had never really taken the time to look at her properly. She was usually just... part of the group. But now, with the soft light filtering through the clouds, her features looked different. Her hazel eyes held a certain warmth, her damp curls framing her face in a way that made her seem...

He blinked and looked away.

Anushka, on the other hand, felt her heart race. It wasn't often that she got a moment alone with Siva. Usually, there was always noise, always someone else around. But right now, it was just them. Just the rain, the quiet, and something unspoken in the air.

She suddenly became aware of how close they were standing, of the way her fingers tightened slightly around the umbrella handle.

The rain began to slow, and with it, the moment faded. The world around them returned to normal.

Siva cleared his throat. "Looks like it's stopping."

Anushka nodded. "Yeah."

An awkward silence settled between them.

Then, they heard voices approaching.

"Yo, you guys alive?" Imtiaz called out, grinning. "We thought you got washed away."

Siva smirked, stepping away from the pillar. "Almost did."

Anushka let out a small laugh, shaking off the last bit of nervousness. Whatever that moment had been, it was gone now.

The next morning...The sunlight filtered through the curtains, casting a soft golden glow across the room. Siva groaned as his alarm buzzed beside him, lazily stretching an arm out to shut it off. He blinked a few times, adjusting to the brightness, and let out a deep sigh before pulling himself up.

It was one of those mornings that felt oddly peaceful, the kind where the world seemed to move a little slower, giving him a moment to breathe. For the first time in weeks, things felt... normal. Or at least as normal as they could be.

He ran a hand through his messy hair, yawning as he swung his legs off the bed. His body was still sore from everything that had happened recently, but it wasn't enough to slow him down. There was too much to do, too many things to balance.

Siva glanced at the other room, where Ayan was still asleep. He had been recovering well, but Siva still made it a habit to check on him first thing in the morning.

Siva padded into the small kitchen, rolling up the sleeves of his t-shirt as he began making a simple breakfast: nothing fancy, just toast, eggs, and some tea. It had become a habit of his, making sure Ayan had something to eat in the morning. It wasn't much, but it was something.

Just as he was setting the plates down on the table, Ayan appeared in the doorway, stretching his arms with a quiet groan. His movements were still slow, but at least he was walking without much trouble.

"You made breakfast?" Ayan asked, rubbing his eyes as he sat down.

Siva smirked. "You sound surprised."

"More like suspicious," Ayan muttered before taking a bite of toast.

Siva leaned on the counter, sipping his tea. "Well, what can I say? I'm a generous guy."

Ayan scoffed. "You still have to pay the rent."

Siva acting shocked "whaaat?"

Ayan rolled his eyes. "You're not getting a free pass just because you decided to play nurse."

Siva let out a dramatic sigh. "Unbelievable. Here I am, offering my noble services, and I still get billed."

Ayan gave him a deadpan look. "Take it or leave it."

Siva grinned. "Fine, fine. But I'm using the big room."

Ayan shot him a glare. "Not happening."

After breakfast, Siva grabbed his bag and slung it over his shoulder.

"I'm heading to college," he said. "You need anything?"

Ayan leaned back in his chair. "Some silence?"

"Sorry, fresh out of stock," Siva shot back.

Ayan smirked slightly. "Then just grab me some snacks on your way back."

Siva gave him a thumbs-up before heading out the door.

By the time Siva arrived at campus, the usual morning chaos was in full swing. Students hurried past, some lost in their notes, others engaged in last-minute cramming. The normalcy of it all felt... grounding.

First stop: the library.

On the way, he ran into Imtiaz and Meenakshi.

"You actually look alive today," Imtiaz remarked.

"Yeah, well, sleep is a luxury," Siva replied.

Meenakshi raised an eyebrow. "Left Ayan's side again? That's two in a row. Should we be worried about a breakup?"

"Haha," Siva said, adjusting his bag. "Don't worry, I left him with enough food to last till I get back."

Imtiaz smirked. "You know, you're starting to sound like his mom."

Siva rolled his eyes. "And yet he still doesn't listen to me."

The three of them laughed before heading toward their classes.

Anushka was already inside the class, her eyes fixed on the door, almost as if she was waiting for someone. She sat with one hand resting under her chin, absentmindedly twirling a pen between her fingers. The usual chatter of students around her faded into the background as her gaze remained steady, anticipation flickering in her expression.

Anushka looked up as Siva settled into his seat. Her eyes flickered to his hand before she met his gaze. "How's your hand?" she asked,

Siva flexed his fingers, glancing down at them. "It's healing pretty good."

She raised an eyebrow. "That's a lie."

Siva smirked. "Fine, maybe it's a little sore, but nothing I can't handle."

Anushka scoffed. "Right, because being reckless is a personality trait for you."

Siva leaned back in his chair. "I prefer to call it 'living life to the fullest.'"

Anushka rolled her eyes. "Yeah, well, try not to 'live' yourself into another hospital stay. I doubt Ayan wants to deal with that."

Siva chuckled. "Noted. No unnecessary heroics...for now."

She shook her head but couldn't quite hide the small smile tugging at her lips. "Good. I'd rather not waste my time checking up on an idiot who doesn't know how to take care of himself."

Siva placed a hand on his chest mockingly. "Wow, Anushka, that almost sounded like you care."

She snorted. "Don't push it." Then, as if deciding she was done with the conversation, she flipped open her notebook and started scribbling something down.

THIRTEEN

THE MAN BEHIND THE MONSTER

Meanwhile, the cold wind howled through the towering trees, their dark silhouettes swaying like restless spirits in the high ranges of Pakistan. The camp, hidden deep within the dense forest, was alive with movement: armed men patrolling the perimeter, low murmurs of hushed conversations, and the occasional sound of crackling firewood breaking the uneasy silence. The scent of damp earth and burning wood filled the air, mixing with the distant echo of a wolf's howl.

In the center of it all, a large tent stood, dimly illuminated by lanterns. Inside, the air was heavy, thick with an unspoken tension. Several men sat in silence, their eyes fixed downward, avoiding the gaze of the one man who could freeze their blood with a single glance...Ibrahim Al-Malik.

He sat at the head of a long wooden table, his broad shoulders casting shadows against the canvas walls. His right eye, clouded and white, gave him an eerie, ghostly presence, while the scar running down the right side of his face made him look like a figure from a nightmare. His long, graying beard rested against his chest as he clasped his hands together, his fingers lightly tapping the wooden surface.

The room remained silent, the weight of his presence suffocating. No one dared to speak unless spoken to. The flickering light cast shadows on his face, making him appear even more terrifying than he already was.

Then, Kabir stepped forward. Unlike the others, he did not lower his gaze. He met Ibrahim's cold stare with unwavering confidence. Clad in black, his face was expressionless, unreadable. His calmness was unsettling to those around him, his presence as feared as the man sitting before him.

Ibrahim exhaled slowly. "Three of our men were captured." His voice was deep, strong, carrying a vibration that sent chills through those present. "This mission was well planned, yet somehow, the authorities knew."

A man to the left swallowed hard. "We...We're looking into how this happened, Malik."

Ibrahim's gaze snapped toward him, and the man instantly lowered his head, his breath hitching.

"We should already know," Ibrahim said, his tone controlled, yet sharp as a blade. "Failures can happen, but failures of this nature?" His fingers tightened around the wooden edge of the table. "They are happening too often."

The silence that followed was deafening. No one moved. No one even dared to breathe too loudly.

Kabir, however, remained unshaken. He folded his arms and spoke, his voice steady. "You suspect a leak."

Ibrahim's expression did not change. "It is a possibility. One that we cannot ignore."

Another man hesitantly spoke, his voice trembling. "We have doubled security. No one..."

Ibrahim raised a hand, silencing him. "Enough." He then turned to Kabir. "I want you to look into this. Find out if there is a leak."

Kabir gave a slow nod. "Understood."

Ibrahim leaned back in his chair, his gaze never leaving Kabir. "Your business with your brother is your own," he said, almost as an afterthought. "But remember... personal matters come second."

Kabir's expression remained unreadable. "I haven't forgotten."

Ibrahim studied him for a moment before nodding slightly. "Good."

The tension in the room remained thick, the air uncomfortably heavy. The meeting had made one thing clear: failures would no longer be tolerated.

Later That Day.

The sun was slowly sinking behind the mountains, casting long shadows across the snow-covered peak. A soft breeze carried the scent of pine and damp earth, the only sound being the occasional rustling of leaves and the distant call of an eagle soaring high above.

A few kilometers from the camp, Kabir sat on a small rock, his gaze fixed on the mountains. His posture was relaxed, yet his presence carried an unsettling stillness. It was impossible to tell what was running through his mind. Was he simply admiring the view, or was he already planning his next move?

Footsteps crunched lightly against the snow. A deep, commanding voice followed.

"I knew I'd find you here."

Kabir didn't turn. He already knew who it was.

Ibrahim stopped a few steps away, looking at the same view before shaking his head. "I know these mountains are beautiful, but I never understood why you stare at them so much."

For a moment, there was only silence. Then, Kabir finally spoke, his voice calm yet carrying a depth of thought.

"Mountains are the greatest illusion of permanence. They stand for centuries, yet with time, even they crumble into dust. Everything that seems immovable eventually falls. The world forgets that."

Ibrahim exhaled, a smirk tugging at the corner of his lips. "Always the philosopher."

Kabir turned slightly, his gaze sharp. "A man who does not think beyond the present is bound to be buried by it."

Ibrahim studied him for a moment before nodding. "We can't have those three spill our plans."

Kabir's expression remained unreadable. "It's already been taken care of."

Ibrahim said nothing, his face giving away no reaction. A lone hawk circled overhead, letting out a sharp cry that echoed across the cliffs. The message was clear..

Ibrahim turned to leave. Kabir remained seated, eyes still locked on the mountains. The world would crumble, eventually. But only fools let it crumble before their work was done.

Back in Mumbai..

The city buzzed with life as the sun dipped below the horizon. The distant honking of cars, the faint murmur of voices, and the occasional howl of a stray dog filled the air. The humidity lingered, clinging to the evening like an unshakable weight.

Inside Ayan's room, the atmosphere was much quieter. Ayan sat on the couch, arms crossed, his expression veiled. The healing bruises on his face had faded, but the turmoil in his mind had not.

"Raghav entered the room, placing a bowl of fruits and a couple of soft drinks on the table in front of Ayan. 'How are you feeling?'"

Ayan barely glanced at it. "Same as yesterday."

Raghav sighed, taking a seat across from him. "You're recovering well. That's good."

Ayan, still staring at the table, spoke without looking up. "Have you gotten anything from the ones you captured? Their locations? Their plans?"

Raghav exhaled slowly, his voice carrying the weight of experience. "Ayan, this is police work. Your focus should be on your studies and getting better."

Ayan's jaw tightened. "You know I can't do that."

Raghav leaned forward, his tone firm but not harsh. "You have a good life ahead of you, Ayan. Stop chasing this. I promise you, Kabir will face justice."

Ayan didn't respond, but his silence spoke volumes.

Before either of them could say anything else, Raghav's phone rang. He picked it up, his expression changing as he listened.

His fingers curled around the phone, his brows furrowing.

After a moment, he ended the call.

Ayan noticed the shift in his demeanor instantly. "What happened?"

Raghav didn't answer immediately. He stood, running a hand over his face before finally speaking.

"The three terrorists... they're dead."

Ayan's eyes snapped up. "What?"

Raghav's voice was grave. "All three of them. Found dead in custody."

A cold silence settled between them.

Ayan sat back, his mind racing.

This wasn't a coincidence.

Someone had made sure they never spoke.

Raghav rushed to the station. The air inside the station was heavy with tension. Officers moved around with a quiet urgency, their voices low as if speaking too loudly would disrupt the fragile order of the night. The dull hum of flickering tube lights cast uneven shadows on the walls, adding to the uneasy atmosphere.

He stepped into the corridor leading to the holding cells, his sharp eyes scanning the scene ahead. The forensic team was already working, dressed in their protective gear, methodically documenting the deaths of the three terrorists. The stench of iron and something unsettling lingered in the air: a scent Raghav had long learned to associate with death.

Inspector Jagdish, a seasoned officer with a thick mustache and weary eyes, approached him with a solemn expression.

"What do we have?" Raghav asked, his voice calm but firm.

Jagdish exhaled, rubbing the back of his neck. "All three, dead. Their throats were slit, precise and deep. We found a small piece of broken glass at the scene."

Raghav frowned. "Glass?"

"Yes, sir. We believe they managed to hide a shard somewhere in their clothing or inside the cell. When they realized interrogation was inevitable, they decided to end their lives rather than risk spilling information."

Raghav's jaw tightened as he glanced toward the lifeless bodies on the floor. The forensic team was carefully collecting evidence, taking pictures, and examining the wounds.

"Are you certain it was suicide?" Raghav asked, his tone edged with skepticism.

Jagdish hesitated for a moment before shaking his head. "We can't say with absolute certainty, but as per our security records, no one had access to their cell except for authorized officers, and the guards didn't report anything suspicious. An inside job is highly unlikely."

Raghav studied the crime scene again,

"Did we manage to get anything out of them before this?"

Jagdish sighed. "No. They barely spoke. No names, no locations, no hints about their larger plans. Whoever they were working for, they were loyal to the end."

Raghav let out a slow breath, rubbing his temple. This was a setback, but not a complete loss.

"At least we stopped the blast in time," he muttered. "And now, we have three fewer terrorists to worry about."

Jagdish nodded. "That's one way to look at it, sir."

The clock ticked 8 PM,

Siva entered the house, stretching his arms after a long day. The house was unusually quiet, except for the faint murmur of Ayan's voice from the living room. He slowed his steps as he heard Ayan's voice, sounding distant and resigned.

"I see. So that's a dead end as well."

There was a soft thud: a phone being placed down. Then, a deep sigh of disappointment.

Siva raised an eyebrow. That tone wasn't good. He stepped forward.

"What happened? Did someone die?" Siva asked casually, expecting maybe some minor frustration about something unrelated.

Ayan lifted his gaze, his expression was hard to read. "Yes," he said. "Not one, three. The terrorists Raghav captured that day."

Siva's breath hitched slightly, his relaxed posture straightening. "What?" His voice was no longer playful: just pure shock. "How?"

Ayan exhaled slowly, rubbing his temple. "They killed themselves inside their cell."

Siva's eyes widened. "Inside the cell? When did this happen?"

"A few hours ago. Maybe three. Raghav got the call and went to check. That was him on the phone just now."

Siva processed the words, his mind racing. Something felt off. He knew Ayan was frustrated, but Siva also understood the deeper implications of this. Three terrorists, all deciding to kill themselves at the same time? Inside a secured police cell? It didn't sit right with him.

"That's... too much of a coincidence, don't you think?" he said slowly. "Three of them, all at the same time? What if it was an inside job?"

Ayan leaned back on the couch, shaking his head. "It's probably not," he replied. "Raghav personally looked into it. The security around them was tight. If someone had helped them, there would've been some kind of sign. But there wasn't."

Siva wasn't convinced. "Still, it doesn't sit right. Maybe someone..."

"This is what terrorists do, Siva." Ayan's tone was calm, but there was a finality to it. "Their mission is more important than their own lives. If they get caught, they don't fight for survival. They don't negotiate. They eliminate themselves before we can get any real information. It's the only thing they know how to do."

Siva frowned, running a hand through his hair. "That's messed up."

Ayan let out a dry chuckle. "That's reality."

For a moment, there was silence. The weight of the conversation lingered in the air, pressing down on both of them.

FOURTEEN

SHIFTING TIDES

The next morning, for the first time in a long while, Ayan returned to college.

He had always refused to sit behind Siva on a bike. But today, for some reason, he was okay with it. Just not on the R15.

"Take the Enfield today," Ayan said, tossing Siva the keys to his bike.

Siva gave him a curious look. "Since when do you let me ride your bike?"

Ayan shrugged, looking away. "Maybe I don't feel like sitting behind that tiny thing of yours."

Siva smirked. "Ohh, I get it. You feel more manly on the Enfield, huh?"

Ayan scoffed. "Just shut up and start the bike."

Still grinning, Siva did as he was told. The deep rumble of the Enfield echoed through the street as Ayan hopped on behind him, gripping the side handles instead of Siva's shoulder.

Maybe he didn't care about the bike. Or maybe he did. Either way, he wasn't about to admit it.

Siva's hand had healed completely, and Ayan was nearly as good as new. They both knew that leaving Ayan alone at home was no longer an option; whether he admitted it or not, he needed to be around people again.

The ride to college was smooth, the cool morning breeze brushing past them as they weaved through the streets. Unlike before, Ayan didn't feel the same weight of suffocation pressing on him. For once, there was no overthinking. No discomfort.

And for the first time ever, Ayan found himself walking toward Siva's group instead of simply watching from a distance.

The gang was gathered in their usual spot outside the main building. Meenakshi and Imtiaz were deep in conversation about something, Anushka was scrolling through her phone, and Arun, who had just arrived, was stretching like he'd just woken up from a year-long nap.

It was Siva who reached them first, but Ayan followed closely behind.

The conversation came to a halt. Eyes turned toward him, not in shock but in simple acknowledgment. There was no pity. No forced enthusiasm. Just recognition.

"Whoa," Arun said, rubbing his eyes. "Did I wake up in the wrong timeline, or is Ayan actually hanging out with us?"

Siva grinned. "I know, right? Feels like the universe shifted or something."

Ayan sighed, shaking his head. "I'm literally just standing here. No need to make it weird."

Meenakshi smirked. "You being here is weird. But in a good way."

Anushka, who had been observing quietly, finally spoke. "How's your arm?"

"It's fine. All healed up", Siva responded.

Anushka nodded. "Good."

There was a beat of silence, but it wasn't uncomfortable.

Imtiaz, ever the peacemaker, finally clapped his hands together. "Alright then! Since this is a historic moment, I say we make it official. Ayan Ali, welcome to the group."

Ayan scoffed. "Don't push it."

The others chuckled, and just like that, the moment passed. The conversations resumed, and Ayan found himself sitting beside Siva, listening to their back-and-forth with quiet interest. He wasn't talkative, but he wasn't distant either.

As they walked through the corridors, the conversations flowed effortlessly. Imtiaz was cracking jokes as usual, making Meenakshi roll her eyes while secretly trying not to laugh. Arun was talking about a football match, and Anushka was debating with him about how cricket was the superior sport.

Ayan didn't contribute much, but he didn't mind. He just sat there, listening, observing. He wasn't used to this, this lightheartedness, this ease.

At lunch, they sat together in the canteen. It was loud, chaotic, but oddly comforting. Ayan still wasn't much of a talker, but every now and then, he responded. A comment here, a short reply there. Small moments, but they mattered.

At one point, he caught Anushka looking at Siva. Not just looking…watching.

The way she smiled at him when he spoke. The way her eyes lingered for just a second too long. The way she leaned slightly closer whenever he laughed.

Ayan smirked. Interesting.

The rest of the day went by surprisingly smoothly. Ayan didn't expect to enjoy it, but… he did.

That night, Ayan and Siva sat on the terrace, the cool air wrapping around them.

Siva was sipping his tea while Ayan leaned back against the railing, staring at the stars. The city hummed in the background, distant and unobtrusive.

After a long silence, Ayan finally spoke.

"So… Anushka, huh?"

Siva, mid-sip, nearly choked on his tea.

"What?" He coughed.

Ayan smirked. "Come on, don't play dumb. Even a blind monkey could tell she's in love with you."

Siva rubbed the back of his neck, glancing away. "You're imagining things."

Ayan tilted his head. "Am I?"

Silence.

"She looks at you like you're her whole damn world, Siva." Ayan continued, his voice calm but certain. "And I know you like her too."

Siva let out a nervous laugh, still avoiding his gaze. "It's complicated."

Ayan immediately picked up on the hesitation. After a brief pause, he said, "You're afraid of commitment, aren't you?"

Siva tensed. He didn't respond right away, just exhaled deeply, watching the steam rise from his cup.

After a long pause, he finally muttered, "It's not that simple."

Ayan remained silent, giving him space to find his words.

Siva sighed. "I'm afraid of love, Ayan."

Ayan frowned but didn't interrupt.

"The love I've seen in my life: it never lasted. It always ended badly." Siva's voice was quieter now. "My father... he was in love once. Or at least, that's what he claimed. But he changed. He became someone else. Love turned to hate, care turned to violence. I watched it happen, and I swore I'd never let myself go through that. I don't want to love someone only to end up hurting them."

Ayan listened carefully, his expression unreadable.

Then, after a moment, he simply said, "You are not your father, Siva."

Siva looked up, his jaw tightening.

Ayan met his gaze firmly. "We choose who we are. Our fathers... their choices do not define us. We define ourselves."

Siva swallowed hard, his fingers tightening around the cup. "I wish I could believe that."

Ayan took a deep breath. "I get it, though. The fear. The weight of something bigger than yourself. But I also know that if you keep running from it, you'll never escape it."

Siva let those words sink in.

Then, after a long silence, he glanced at Ayan. "And what about you?"

Ayan raised an eyebrow. "What about me?"

Siva hesitated, then said, "You've been living your life for one thing, revenge. Every moment, every breath has been about finding him and killing him. But is that really living?"

Ayan froze. The words hit him harder than he expected.

Siva continued, "You said I shouldn't let my father define me. But aren't you letting Kabir define you?"

Ayan let out a dry chuckle. "Damn. You're getting good at this."

Siva smirked slightly, but his eyes held something deeper: concern.

Ayan exhaled slowly, rubbing his fingers together before finally answering. "You're right." He looked up at the sky, as if searching for something in the stars. "I've spent my whole life chasing him. Every second, every thought. But no matter what I do, it never feels like enough."

He paused, then said, "So, I decided... I'll give life a chance."

Siva blinked in surprise. "Wait, really?"

Ayan smirked. "Don't get too excited. That doesn't mean I'm letting go of my goal. I'm still going after him."

Siva rolled his eyes. "Of course."

Ayan's expression softened. "But I realized something. In order to beat him, I have to be better than him. And you... You made me realize how."

Siva frowned. "How?"

Ayan smiled faintly. "By living."

Siva opened his mouth to protest, but Ayan cut him off. "I'm not the kind of guy to talk about love or all that nonsense, but... I've seen the way Anushka looks at you. Her care is genuine. She's not like your father or your past. She's your present. And maybe... your future."

Siva swallowed hard, looking away. "I don't know if I can."

Ayan's voice was quiet, but firm. "You won't know unless you try."

Siva let out a deep breath. "You make it sound so easy."

Ayan smirked. "It's not. Nothing worth it ever is."

FIFTEEN

ANCHOR POINTS

The ceiling fan groaned above Ayan's head as he lay sprawled across his bed, textbook propped against his knees. Finals loomed in five days, and though he'd never admit it, the collective panic had seeped into him too. Across the room, Siva sat cross-legged on the floor, surrounded by a fortress of highlighted notes and empty energy drink cans.

"You realize caffeine doesn't actually make you smarter," Ayan remarked, watching Siva rub his temples.

"It makes me feel smarter," Siva muttered, squinting at his physics equations. "Which is basically the same thing."

Ayan snorted and returned to his books. The silence stretched comfortably until Siva's phone buzzed: a flurry of messages lighting up the screen.

"Group chat's on fire," Siva said, grinning as he scrolled. "Imtiaz just found out there's a closed-book section in the law paper. He's threatening to drop out and become a goat farmer."

"Goats are smarter than him," Ayan said, though the corner of his mouth twitched.

Siva tapped out a reply, then hesitated. "Anushka says she's got extra notes if we want to study at the library tomorrow."

Ayan flipped a page. "We?"

"Come on," Siva wheedled. "You've been holed up here for days. Even assassins take bathroom breaks."

The library was quieter the next morning, sunlight streaming through high windows onto long wooden tables. Anushka had already claimed a corner, her notes color-coded with an intensity that bordered on militaristic. She looked up as they approached, a pencil tucked behind her ear.

"You're late," she said, though her eyes crinkled at the edges.

Siva collapsed into the chair beside her. "Blame His Highness here. He ironed his socks."

"I did not," Ayan said, too quickly.

Anushka hid a laugh behind her hand as Siva gasped in delight. "You did! Look at his face!"

Ayan pointedly ignored them, unpacking his books with exaggerated precision. But as the hours passed, he found himself drawn into their rhythm: Siva's dramatic groans over calculus, Anushka's patient explanations, the way she'd tap her pencil against the table when thinking. At one point, she leaned across to correct Siva's equation, her hair brushing his arm. Siva froze, his ears turning pink. Ayan rolled his eyes and tossed a wadded-up napkin at him.

It didn't take much time for Siva to give up. He slammed his physics textbook shut with a groan. "I swear, if I have to calculate one more projectile motion, I'm jumping out that window."

Anushka smirked without looking up from her notes. "You'd miss the ground because you forgot to account for gravity."

"Ouch," Imtiaz chuckled, tossing a peanut at Siva's head. "Even Anushka's roasting you now."

The next few days slipped by in a blur, and finally, the day had arrived...

The Physics exam hall was steeped in silence, save for the scratching of pens and the occasional cough. The weight of final exams had turned even the most indifferent students into desperate scribblers, hunched over their answer sheets as if their futures depended on each stroke of ink.

Ayan sat three rows from the front, his hand gliding effortlessly over the pages. His expression remained calm, but his focus was razor-sharp: every number, every formula etched into his mind with mechanical precision. Three rows ahead, Siva was a different story.

His knee bounced uncontrollably under the desk, his fingers fidgeting with the pen cap. He shifted in his seat, shot a glance at the clock, and suppressed the urge to groan. Fifteen minutes left.

From across the room, Anushka caught his eye and subtly tapped her wristwatch twice: their silent signal from countless study sessions. Check your time, idiot.

Siva exhaled through his nose, then gave a dramatic wipe of his forehead, mouthing, I'm dying. Anushka pressed her lips together, trying not to laugh.

When the final bell rang, Siva practically stumbled out of the exam hall, arms flailing as if escaping a battlefield.

"That was absolute murder." He collapsed onto the grass outside, eyes squeezed shut. "I think I just failed my entire future."

Anushka sat beside him, her checked shirt half-tucked into high-waisted jeans, sleeves rolled up just enough to show off her watch. "Let me see your rough work."

She reached for his answer sheet, their fingers brushing for half a second too long. A tiny, unnoticed shift in the air. Siva's breath hitched.

She scanned the page. "It's not that bad," she said with a small smile. "Surprisingly, it looks like you actually studied."

Ayan, leaning against the neem tree a few feet away, observed the exchange in silence. "At least you remembered there were formulas involved this time," he remarked dryly.

Siva groaned and chucked a guava at him.

Ayan caught it one-handed. "I take it back. Your aim's improving. Must be all that physics finally sinking in."

That night, their study session dissolved into chaos when Imtiaz discovered Siva's so-called "cheat sheet": a single, wrinkled post-it note with the words THINK HARD scrawled in block letters.

"You're joking," Meenakshi deadpanned, holding it up.

"It's philosophical," Siva defended, leaning back smugly. "A reminder that...

"That you're an idiot," Imtiaz finished.

Anushka shook her head but smiled despite herself. Absentmindedly, she reached over to straighten Siva's collar, only to freeze mid-motion. The realization of her gesture hit them both at the same time.

Siva's ears turned pink.

"You're hopeless," she muttered, voice softer than intended.

Siva didn't argue.

From the periphery of the group, Ayan watched, saying nothing. But the corner of his mouth twitched: almost a smile.

A few weeks later,

The notice board was practically under siege. Students pushed and shoved, desperate to glimpse their fate.

Siva had a death grip on Anushka's wrist as they fought their way forward.

"There!" She pointed at his name. "You passed everything!"

Siva whooped so loudly that a few birds abandoned their perch in nearby trees. Without thinking, he grabbed Anushka and spun her in a circle, her feet momentarily leaving the ground.

The moment his hands landed on her waist, the rush of adrenaline faded into something else. She was close, closer than she'd ever been before. Her hands rested against his chest, fingers lightly curled.

Neither of them moved.

The air between them thickened, stretched, until Arun crashed into them with a bear hug.

"GOA TRIP IS ON!"

Anushka quickly stepped back, smoothing her hair. Siva rubbed the back of his neck, suddenly unable to meet her eyes.

From a few feet away, Ayan caught Siva's glance and gave a slight, almost imperceptible nod. His version of encouragement.

The following Friday, on their journey to Goa.

The train smelled of rust and overripe bananas. Siva had somehow maneuvered his way next to Anushka, their shoulders lightly brushing as the train swayed.

"Remember that time in first year," she mused suddenly, "when you set the chemistry lab on fire?"

Siva gasped. "First of all, it was a controlled flare-up. Second...

"Second," Ayan interrupted from across the aisle, not even looking up, "you screamed like a banshee and hid behind Professor Menon."

The entire compartment erupted in laughter.

Anushka's hand landed on Siva's arm as she laughed, and neither of them moved it when the laughter faded.

The reality of the homestay was a bit different than what they expected. The villa in Goa was a disaster: peeling paint, a ceiling fan that groaned like a dying animal, and a suspicious stain on Imtiaz's mattress.

"Five stars," Siva declared, flopping onto the sagging couch. A spring burst through with a sad ping.

Anushka opened the balcony doors, letting the salty air in. "We're five minutes from the beach. We should check it out now!"

"Lunch first," Siva reminded. "Or we'll pass out before reaching the water."

The group agreed and stepped out into the bustling Goan streets, filled with the smell of seafood, the distant sound of live music, and tourists bargaining at stalls.

At a small restaurant, the real challenge began: ordering food.

Imtiaz pointed at a dish on the menu. "This one sounds good."

The waiter raised an eyebrow. "Sir, that's a seafood platter. You said you were allergic to prawns."

Imtiaz paled. "Right. Never mind."

Anushka nudged Siva. "Try the Goan fish curry."

"I'll just eat whatever you order," he said without thinking.

She paused, then smiled. "Noted."

By the time they reached the shore, the sky was a mix of orange and pink. The sea stretched endlessly, waves curling at their feet.

Anushka was the first to run in, laughing as the water splashed around her.

Siva followed. "Ayan, let's go!"

Ayan stood at the edge, the cold water touching his toes. He wasn't afraid of the ocean; he just didn't see the point.

Still, after a long pause, he stepped forward.

Siva grinned. "Attaboy."

For a while, they just existed: the sound of waves, the scent of salt, the feeling of wet sand beneath their feet.

Meenakshi and Anushka collected seashells, while Imtiaz and Arun attempted to build a sandcastle...and failed.

At some point, Anushka turned toward the horizon.

"I wish time would slow down," she murmured.

Siva, standing beside her, glanced at her profile. "Why?"

She shrugged. "Good moments don't last long."

Siva's smile faltered.

Later that night, after dinner, they built a small bonfire on the beach. The warmth flickered against their faces, casting shadows in the sand.

Siva stretched his arms. "Okay, ghost stories time."

"No," Ayan said instantly.

Imtiaz ignored him. "I know a true one."

Anushka smirked. "Let me guess: about a haunted hotel?"

"No, this one's worse," Imtiaz leaned forward, lowering his voice. "A couple came to Goa for their honeymoon. But on the first night, the husband disappeared."

Siva frowned. "And?"

"They say the wife kept hearing whispers, and every time she turned, she saw his reflection in the mirror, smiling."

Anushka rolled her eyes. "That's just a bad horror movie plot."

"Hey, believe what you want," Imtiaz said. "But I wouldn't look at any mirrors tonight."

Siva and Anushka exchanged amused glances. Ayan, unimpressed, tossed a small rock into the fire.

Siva glanced at him. "You don't scare easily, huh?"

Ayan's expression didn't change. "I've seen worse things than ghosts."

Silence.

The lightness of the moment shifted.

Siva, sensing the change, nudged Ayan's shoulder. "Then maybe you should tell the next story."

Ayan just looked at the flames, saying nothing.

By midnight, everyone headed back to the villa.

Ayan lay in bed, staring at the ceiling. Sleep never came easily. His mind was too full, too restless.

He sat up, quietly stepping out onto the balcony. The ocean shimmered under the moonlight, waves moving endlessly.

The villa felt too confined. Too warm. Too unfamiliar.

He needed air.

Silently, he slipped out of bed, grabbed his jacket, and walked out onto the dimly lit street. The air smelled of salt and earth, and the sky above stretched in an endless blanket of stars.

His feet moved on their own, leading him toward the beach.

The sand was cool beneath his feet, the grains shifting with each slow step. The ocean stretched out before him: vast, endless, unknowable.

This was why he preferred the night.

No tourists. No noise. Just him and the sea.

Ayan walked toward the water, stopping just where the waves lapped at the shore. He let his shoes sink into the wet sand as he watched the rhythmic pull of the tide.

The sea had always fascinated him. It was calm, yet merciless. It took what it wanted.

Just like Kabir.

Ayan exhaled sharply, closing his eyes.

Kabir.

The name alone stirred something bitter inside him.

Even now, after all these years, he couldn't escape him. His voice. His presence. The weight of his actions.

He opened his eyes, staring at the waves as if they held answers.

Why had he come on this trip?

Because Siva wouldn't stop pestering him?

Because it was easier to say yes than argue?

Or maybe…just maybe…he wanted to know what it felt like to live.

To be a normal college student.

To laugh. To breathe.

But he knew better. Some people weren't meant for normal.

He clenched his fists, feeling the rough texture of sand between his fingers.

The silence of the beach was both comforting and suffocating.

The next morning, the sun hung high in the sky, its golden light bouncing off the endless waves of the Arabian Sea. The beach was buzzing with life: families laughing, vendors selling coconut water, and the occasional stray dog trotting along the shore in search of food.

Ayan walked alongside the group, hands in his pockets, half-listening as they chatted around him. Siva, as usual, was the loudest, animatedly pitching the idea of swimming or trying out some water sports today..

"We're literally at the beach! What's the point if we don't even get in the water?" Siva said, waving his arms for emphasis.

"Some of us came here to relax, not drown," Meenakshi muttered.

"Drown?" Arun scoffed. "Meenakshi, do you even know how to swim?"

She gave Him a flat stare. "I know enough not to die."

"That's not very convincing."

Before Meenakshi could continue, Anushka spoke up. "Boating sounds fun."

Siva's face lit up. "See? That's the spirit! Let's rent one!"

A little over an hour later, the group was on a speedboat, cutting through the waves as the salty wind lashed against their faces.

Siva was at the front, arms spread wide. "I feel like a movie hero right now!"

"More like an idiot," Imtiaz muttered, shaking his head.

Anushka sat near the railing, her hands gripping the metal bars as she watched the waves.

The boat rocked gently at first, the driver keeping a steady pace. But as they went further into the sea, the waves grew rougher. The boat jolted every few seconds, splashing water onto their clothes.

"Okay, maybe this wasn't the best idea," Meenakshi said, clutching the seat beside her.

"Relax," Siva said, turning to face them. "It's just a little...

The boat lurched.

Hard.

And before anyone could react, Anushka lost her balance.

Her foot slipped against the wet surface. Her hands barely brushed the railing, but she missed.

And then...

She fell.

The splash was loud.

For a moment, no one moved. The shock of what had just happened left them frozen.

Then,

"ANUSHKA!"

Siva's voice snapped through the air, panic lacing every syllable.

Ayan stood up immediately, eyes scanning the waves.

Nothing.

She wasn't surfacing.

"Shit... Siva didn't think. He just jumped.

The water was colder than expected, a sharp contrast to the warm air. The current was stronger than it had looked from the boat, dragging him downward.

He forced himself deeper, eyes burning as he searched.

And then, he saw her.

Anushka's body was sinking, her arms struggling weakly against the pull of the sea.

Without hesitation, he swam toward her, reaching for her wrist. Her movements were slowing.

She was running out of air.

Siva grabbed her and pulled her against him, kicking his legs with everything he had. His lungs screamed for oxygen, but he didn't stop. He couldn't.

After what felt like an eternity, they broke the surface.

"ANUSHKA!" he gasped, shaking her slightly.

Her head lolled to the side.

She wasn't breathing.

The others pulled them back onto the boat, their faces pale with fear.

"Is she... Meenakshi's voice cracked.

"She's not breathing," Ayan said, his tone eerily calm.

Siva's hands shook as he placed her down. "Shit, shit, shit...

He tilted her head back.

One breath.

Nothing.

Another breath.

Then...a cough.

Water spilled from Anushka's lips as she gasped for air, her chest heaving.

A collective breath of relief washed over the boat.

Siva let out a breath he hadn't realized he was holding.

"You scared the hell out of me," he muttered.

Anushka's eyes slowly opened, unfocused.

And then, she looked at him.

For a second, neither of them spoke. The world around them blurred.

Their faces were too close. The heat of her breath ghosted over his lips.

And then, she kissed him.

Soft. Quick. But real.

Siva froze.

Anushka pulled away just as quickly, her cheeks flushed, not just from exhaustion.

The others said nothing.

Ayan just looked away.

"We should head back," he said flatly.

And just like that, the moment was gone.

The boat ride back was quiet. Not the comfortable kind of silence, but the heavy, loaded kind. The kind that came when something shifted, when words hovered in the air but no one knew how to say them.

She could still feel the ghost of Siva's lips on hers. The heat of his touch. The moment had felt right: in the adrenaline, in the relief of being alive, but now...

Had she crossed a line?

Her stomach twisted.

Siva had saved her, pulled her out of the water with such desperation in his eyes. She hadn't even thought; she had just felt. And now, sitting beside him on the boat, the reality of what she had done started to sink in.

She snuck a glance at him.

He was staring straight ahead, his usual carefree grin absent. His shirt was still damp, his hair messy from the wind. He hadn't said a word about the kiss. Hadn't even looked at her properly.

Anushka swallowed. Maybe I shouldn't have.

The thought made her heart sink.

She licked her lips, suddenly nervous. "Siva...

He turned to her at once, like he had been waiting for her to speak. His gaze was steady, blank.

She hesitated, her fingers curling into the fabric of her dress. "I... I think I got caught up in the moment. I didn't mean to... She exhaled sharply, shaking her head. "I wasn't thinking, and if that made you uncomfortable, I'm sorry."

Siva's brows furrowed, and for a second, he looked almost offended.

"Uncomfortable?" His voice was quiet, rough around the edges.

Anushka looked away.

"I just don't want things to be weird between us," she muttered.

There was a beat of silence. Then, she felt the boat shift slightly as Siva turned toward her completely.

"Anushka."

Something in his voice made her glance up.

His eyes, dark and hard to read just moments ago, were filled with something else now. Something fierce.

Before she could process it, he reached out.

His hand cupped her cheek, fingers still slightly cool from the water. Her breath caught.

"You think I didn't want that?" His voice was quieter now, lower.

Anushka's lips parted, but no words came out.

"I was just giving you a chance to take it back."

She barely had time to react before he leaned in, closing the space between them.

His lips pressed against hers, warm and sure, and for a second, she forgot how to breathe.

Then, her body reacted before her mind could catch up.

She kissed him back.

This wasn't like the first time. There was no rush, no chaos. It was slow, lingering, like they were both trying to memorize the moment.

Somewhere behind them, someone let out a loud whistle.

"Finally!" Imtiaz called out, laughing.

Meenakshi groaned. "Took you two long enough."

Siva pulled away just enough to rest his forehead against hers, his grin returning.

"Guess we're not very subtle," he muttered.

Anushka, still breathless, let out a soft laugh. "Not at all."

And just like that, the tension melted.

The others cheered, teasing them relentlessly, but Siva didn't care.

He kept his hand on hers as they rode back to shore, the sun dipping below the horizon, painting the sky in shades of gold and crimson.

And for once, everything felt exactly as it should be.

The following morning was more pleasant than the previous one. The waves rolled lazily onto the shore, their rhythmic hum blending with the distant laughter of tourists and the occasional squawk of seagulls. The villa, though still unimpressive, now carried a certain charm in the warm light, like a safe haven tucked away from reality.

Siva stretched his arms as he stepped out onto the small balcony, the salty air filling his lungs. Below, Anushka stood barefoot in the sand, her hair tousled by the wind as she watched the waves.

A small smile crept onto his lips.

"Morning," he called.

She turned, smiling softly. "You're up early."

"I could say the same for you," he teased, hopping down the stairs.

"Couldn't sleep much," she admitted. "Still thinking about yesterday."

Siva's chest tightened, but before he could say anything, she took his hand and gave it a light squeeze. "In a good way."

That was all he needed to hear.

He grinned. "Well, then... shall we make today just as memorable?"

The day blurred into a series of moments: small, quiet ones that felt too perfect to be real.

Breakfast was a slow, lazy affair, with Anushka stealing food from Siva's plate and him retaliating with dramatic protests.

"Why do you always take my toast?" he groaned as she popped a piece into her mouth.

"It tastes better when it's stolen."

"That's criminal behavior."

"Then arrest me," she teased, nudging his foot under the table.

Later, they strolled through the beachside market, weaving through the crowd, Siva's hand resting lightly on the small of her back. He bought her a silver anklet from an old street vendor, clasping it around her ankle as she balanced on one foot.

"Now you can't run away," he murmured.

Anushka smirked. "Wouldn't dream of it."

They spent the afternoon out at sea again, but this time, there was no chaos, no fear. Just laughter and splashing as Anushka pulled Siva into the water, both of them tumbling into the waves.

While Siva and Anushka basked in their newfound closeness, Ayan sat in the villa, his focus narrowed on the dim glow of his laptop screen.

The sound of Siva's laughter drifted in from outside, but he barely registered it. His fingers tapped rhythmically against the keyboard, scrolling through articles, reports, old police files, everything he could find on Kabir.

SIXTEEN

BETRAYAL RUNS DEEP

The room was dimly lit, the stale air thick with sweat and blood. Two Indian commandos, Captain Vikram Singh and Lt. Arjun Shekhawat, sat slumped against the wall, their hands bound behind their backs. Two weeks of captivity had left them bruised, beaten, and exhausted. But they had given nothing.

In front of them stood two of Ibrahim's men. One of them idly spun a knife between his fingers, while the other leaned forward, his voice laced with frustration.

"Let's try this again." He crouched before Vikram, gripping his jaw roughly. "How did your army get intel on our attack plans?"

Vikram stared back, silent.

The interrogator sighed, as if dealing with a stubborn child. He turned to his companion. "Bring the photos."

The other man pulled out a thick envelope, tossing it onto the table. Slowly, deliberately, he began spreading out photographs.

Vikram's wife and daughter. Arjun's parents. Their homes. All taken from a close distance.

"Beautiful families," the interrogator mused. "You must miss them." He picked up a photo of Vikram's eight-year-old daughter, running her fingers through her mother's hair. "Shame if something happened to them."

Arjun's jaw clenched.

"Last chance," the man continued. "Tell us how your army found out about our operations, and your families will live."

Still, silence.

The interrogator's smile dropped.

"You think this is a game?" He leaned in closer. "We know where they sleep, where they shop. Where your children play. You can handle pain, but can they?"

A dark pause filled the room.

Then Vikram exhaled, his voice steady.

"You can kill us." His swollen eyes burned with defiance. "You can kill our families. It doesn't matter."

Arjun nodded, spitting blood onto the floor. "We'd rather sacrifice them than betray our nation."

The interrogators stilled.

For a moment, the only sound in the room was the flickering of the lone lightbulb.

Then, a voice cut through the silence.

"Enough."

The door creaked open. Ibrahim stepped inside, followed closely by Kabir.

The interrogators immediately stepped aside, their expressions shifting to unease.

Ibrahim's presence was suffocating. He moved with an air of absolute control, his scarred face twisted into something close to amusement. His one good eye studied the two prisoners, his blind one unmoving.

He let out a slow chuckle.

"Two weeks." He shook his head. "That's impressive. Most don't last half that."

Neither of the commandos responded.

Ibrahim crouched before them, his voice turning almost soothing.

"I will make this simple." He spread his hands. "I will let you go."

Vikram's bruised brow furrowed.

"Yes," Ibrahim continued. "I will drop you off at your homes today. Your families will be waiting, untouched. You will walk free, and this nightmare will be over."

Arjun scoffed. "And all we have to do is betray our country?"

Ibrahim smiled.

"No, Lieutenant," he said softly. "Your country has already been betrayed."

The words hung in the air like a curse.

Vikram's fingers curled into fists. "What are you talking about?"

Ibrahim sighed as if speaking to fools.

"You still believe your borders are protected?" His voice dripped with mockery. "By whom?"

He tilted his head, watching their faces.

"The ones you report to... reports to me."

Arjun's breath hitched.

Ibrahim grinned.

"How do you think we come and go as we please? How do you think our operations remain untouched? You still believe your nation is impenetrable?"

Silence.

For the first time, doubt flickered in their eyes.

Ibrahim's smile widened.

"So, let me ask again... are you willing to cooperate?"

Vikram spat blood onto the floor. "No."

Without hesitation, Ibrahim pulled the knife from his hip,

and sliced Vikram's throat in one smooth motion.

Arjun's eyes widened in horror as his comrade let out a choked gasp, his body convulsing as blood spilled onto the floor.

Vikram collapsed.

Dead.

Arjun's breathing turned erratic, his mind racing.

"W-wait!" he stammered, panic creeping into his voice.

Ibrahim tilted his head, unimpressed.

"The time for talking has passed."

Without another word, he drove the knife into Arjun's throat.

His body jerked violently before going still, blood pooling beneath him.

Ibrahim wiped the blade clean.

"I do not give second chances."

He turned to Kabir, who had watched the entire scene unfold without flinching.

"Ensure their bodies send a message to our enemies in India," Ibrahim ordered

Kabir nodded.

The next morning,

The train rattled along the tracks, cutting through the vast countryside as the golden hues of dusk settled over the horizon. Inside the compartment, the atmosphere was lively; Siva and Anushka sat close, her head resting against his shoulder as they murmured to each other, lost in their world. Imtiaz and Arun were engaged in a fierce game of cards, their voices rising in playful arguments, while Meenakshi leaned against the window, earphones plugged in, nodding along to some old Bollywood song.

Ayan, however, was elsewhere.

He sat by the window, his arms crossed, gaze fixed on the landscape rushing past. The world outside was a blur of green fields and distant hills, but his mind wasn't on the scenery. His thoughts had wandered...back to the nights in the library, back to the countless hours spent searching for Kabir, back to the questions that had no answers.

The train slowed as it approached Ratnagiri Station, the wheels screeching slightly before coming to a halt. Passengers stretched, some stepping out for a breath of fresh air, while vendors hurried along the platform, selling everything from tea to snacks.

And then, a voice pierced through the station's usual noise. Sharp, urgent.

"Fresh news! Fresh news! Two army officers' bodies found near Marina Beach! Potential terrorist attack!"

Ayan's body went rigid. His ears rang.

Without thinking, he shot up from his seat and rushed toward the open doors. His heart pounded in his chest as he stepped onto the platform, searching. There...a boy, no older than sixteen, holding a stack of newspapers high above his head.

"Give me one," Ayan said breathlessly, snatching a copy.

His eyes scanned the bold headline.

"TWO INDIAN COMMANDOS BRUTALLY EXECUTED: LINKS TO TERROR SUSPECTED"

His grip on the paper tightened.

The article detailed how the bodies of Captain Vikram Singh and Lt. Arjun Shekhawat were discovered early that morning, dumped near Marina Beach. Both had been missing for over two weeks. Authorities suspected a larger terror operation at play but had yet to confirm further details.

Ayan's jaw clenched as he read further.

Both officers were key figures in ongoing counter-terrorism investigations. Sources claim they were deeply involved in tracking a certain high-profile militant.

Ayan didn't need to read between the lines.

He already knew.

Kabir.

His hands trembled slightly as he reached for his phone and dialed the one number he knew would have answers.

Raghav.

The phone rang twice before a gruff voice answered.

"Ayan? You alright?"

Ayan didn't waste time. "The news...about the officers. Was it Kabir?"

There was a heavy pause on the other end. A sigh. Then, "Most likely."

Ayan's grip tightened around his phone. "Who were they?"

"Captain Vikram and Lt. Arjun," Raghav said, his voice quieter now. "They were leading officers in the cases against Kabir. If they're dead, it means Kabir knew exactly who was after him."

Ayan inhaled sharply. "Then it's not just an attack. It's a message."

Raghav sighed again. "It is. And Ayan... I don't know much right now. I don't have access to my old Intel anymore. But trust me, if this were Kabir's work, it won't stop here."

Ayan's fists clenched. "It never does."

The train let out a long whistle, signaling departure.

Raghav's voice softened. "Let me get more details, and will discuss once you are back."

Ayan didn't respond.

As the train lurched forward, he stepped back inside, clutching the newspaper like a lifeline. He glanced toward his friends: Siva was laughing as Anushka nudged him playfully, Imtiaz was still caught up in his game, the world around them untouched by the news that had just shattered Ayan's mind.

He sank back into his seat, staring at the blurred scenery once more.

By afternoon, the train finally pulled into Chhatrapati Shivaji Terminus. The station was as chaotic as ever: passengers rushed to and fro, porters hauled heavy luggage, and the sounds of train whistles and announcements filled the air.

Ayan and the gang stepped onto the platform, the warmth of Mumbai settling over them like a familiar weight.

"Back to reality," Meenakshi sighed, stretching her arms.

"Yeah, vacation's over," Arun added, adjusting his bag.

Siva and Anushka, however, lingered. Their hands brushed against each other, neither willing to say bye.

"See you tomorrow?" Anushka asked softly, looking up at Siva.

He grinned. "Obviously. We'll make up for lost time."

She rolled her eyes playfully. "Lost time? We were literally together the whole trip."

"Exactly. Now I'm used to it. Can't just stop," he said, nudging her shoulder.

She laughed, shaking her head. "Idiot."

Meanwhile, Ayan adjusted the strap of his bag and turned to Siva. "Go to the room. I'll meet you there soon."

Siva frowned. "Where are you going?"

"Raghav's house. I need to ask him something."

Siva studied his face for a moment, but Ayan's expression was Unfathomable. Finally, Siva sighed. "Alright, don't take too long."

With that, they parted ways: Ayan heading toward Raghav's house, while the rest of the gang dispersed into the busy city streets.

Ayan stood in front of the familiar house, taking a deep breath before ringing the doorbell.

A few seconds later, Raghav opened the door. His sharp eyes landed on Ayan, and he immediately stepped aside. "Come in."

Ayan entered, the scent of old books and black coffee filling the air. Raghav's house had always been the same: dimly lit, cluttered with case files, and eerily quiet.

They walked to the living room, where Raghav gestured for Ayan to sit. "I assume this is about the two officers."

Ayan nodded, placing the newspaper on the table. "I need to know everything, Raghav. Who were they? What were they investigating?"

Raghav leaned back in his chair, rubbing his temple. "Their names were Vikram Singh and Arjun Shekhawat. They were leading officers in the task force that took over Kabir's case after I retired."

Ayan's fingers tightened into a fist. "And now they're dead."

"Yes," Raghav admitted, his voice grim. "And I believe they dug too deep. That's why they were killed."

Ayan leaned forward. "What do you mean?"

Raghav exhaled slowly before continuing. "These two officers were working undercover. They didn't inform the head of the Anti-Terrorism Squad about their last mission, as it was top secret and delicate. That means we don't know what their final discovery was."

Ayan clenched his jaw. "So we have nothing?"

Raghav shook his head. "Not exactly. Before they disappeared, their last report mentioned something troubling."

Ayan's breath hitched. "What did it say?"

Raghav's eyes darkened. "Kabir is not the head of this organization. He's taking orders from someone else."

Silence fell between them.

Ayan stared at him, his mind racing. "You're telling me... there's someone above Kabir?"

Raghav nodded. "And I believe he is more dangerous than Kabir himself."

Ayan's body tensed, the implications sinking in. For years, he had thought Kabir was the monster at the top: the man responsible for everything. But now... this changed everything.

Someone more dangerous than Kabir.

Someone, Kabir himself, answered to.

And if Vikram and Arjun had uncovered that truth, it meant they had been silenced for it.

Ayan swallowed hard. "Do we know who he is?"

Raghav shook his head. "Not yet. But if Kabir is following someone, it means this organization is bigger than we thought. This isn't just about revenge anymore, Ayan. This is a war."

Ayan exhaled slowly, his fingers gripping the armrest of the chair. His world had just shifted again, and the path ahead was darker than ever.

The weight of his conversation with Raghav still sat heavy on Ayan's mind as he returned to the apartment later that night. The discussion had left him with more questions than answers, his thoughts a storm of frustration and unease.

Days passed, but the lingering tension in Ayan's chest didn't fade. He had spent his time researching, piecing together information about the case, about Kabir. The world moved on, but his mind remained fixed on one thing: revenge.

Then, one evening, he returned to the apartment to find the others gathered around the living room. It had been a while since they had all been in the same place together; Siva was sprawled out on the couch, flipping through his phone, while Anushka sat at the dining table with a notebook open, scribbling things down. Imtiaz leaned against the wall, arms crossed, while Meenakshi tapped on her phone. The air was filled with an unusual energy, one that Ayan hadn't felt in a long time.

"Finally, he arrives," Imtiaz said, looking up.

Ayan raised an eyebrow. "What are you all doing in my apartment?"

"Technically, it's also Siva's," Anushka pointed out without looking up from her notes.

"Still doesn't answer my question."

Siva stretched, grinning. "Relax, man. We're just planning something."

"For what?"

"Siva's birthday," Meenakshi answered, glancing up at Ayan.

Ayan looked at Siva, who simply shrugged.

Before Ayan could say anything, Imtiaz spoke up. "We were thinking of something fun, maybe a weekend getaway somewhere?"

"Or we could rent a place and throw a proper party," Anushka suggested. "One of those rooftop ones with lights and music."

Meenakshi nodded. "Or even something simple, like a dinner at a nice restaurant?"

Siva chuckled, his voice warm and sincere. "I know we usually do this in the evening, with cake, music, and everything, but this year, I'd really like to spend the whole day at the orphanage with the kids. Would that be okay with you all?"

Meenakshi tilted her head. "We do that, right? You spend a few hours in the orphanage in the morning, and then we party at night."

"Yeah, but this year, why don't we all spend the entire day at the orphanage?" Siva suggested with a gentle smile. "Just a calm day: no loud music, no big party. Just us and the kids. We can cook for them, play with them, talk to them... just make it a special day for them. What do you guys think?"

For a moment, there was silence. Then, one by one, smiles began to spread across their faces.

"That's... actually really sweet," Anushka said softly, "I like that idea. I'm in."

"Me too," Meenakshi agreed.

Arun and Imtiaz exchanged glances before nodding. "We're okay with it too, I guess," Imtiaz said.

Siva's gaze landed on Ayan, a playful smirk on his lips. "I'm not gonna ask you because you don't have a choice."

Ayan sighed. "Mm. Fine."

Siva grinned, satisfied. It wasn't just about spending time with the kids; it was also about Ayan. Siva had seen the way he had been on edge lately. Maybe this was his way of grounding him, even if he wouldn't say it out loud.

The morning of Siva's birthday unfolded gently, sunlight spilling over the orphanage as he and the group stepped through its gates. The building wasn't grand; just a simple home for children who had nowhere else to go. But to Siva, it was more than that: it was the place that had raised him, shaped him, and given him a family when he had none.

The moment they stepped inside, the excited chatter of children filled the air. Within seconds, the kids spotted Siva, and the entire place erupted into cheers.

"Siva bhaiyya!" they called out, their small feet racing toward him.

Before Siva could even react, at least five kids threw themselves at him, hugging him tightly.

"Happy Birthday, Siva bhaiyya!" they all shouted in unison.

Siva laughed, lifting one of the younger boys effortlessly into his arms. "Thank you, thank you! You guys are the best."

A little girl, no older than six, tugged at Siva's sleeve and looked up at him with wide, curious eyes. "Bhaiyya, which one is Anushka Didi?"

Siva blinked, feeling all eyes suddenly on him. He let out a nervous chuckle, scratching the back of his head. "How about you guess?" he asked, hoping to shift the attention away.

The girl turned her head, scanning the group with a thoughtful expression before pointing straight at Anushka. "This one!"

Anushka, caught off guard, blushed instantly. The others looked between her and Siva, grinning in amusement.

Meenakshi raised an eyebrow, smirking. "How did you know?"

The little girl grinned. "Because Bhaiyya always talks about her! And she looks exactly like how he describes her!"

Siva's face turned red in an instant. He let out a dramatic sigh, shaking his head with a playful smile. "That's it. You are not supposed to speak again today!" he said, crossing his arms.

The girl giggled, hiding behind Anushka as the group erupted into laughter.

Siva turned to the others, waving his hands dismissively. "She's just making things up, don't listen to her."

Arun smirked, shaking his head. "Yeah, yeah, we get that."

Siva groaned, covering his face as the teasing continued, while Anushka tried (and failed) to fight off her shy smile.

The laughter from the little girl's innocent remark still echoed as they walked deeper into the orphanage. The children, thrilled by Siva and his friends' presence, pulled them in different directions: some eager to show off their drawings, others asking them to play. The air was filled with the kind of warmth that couldn't be bought, only felt.

Siva knelt beside a group of kids playing with handmade toys and ruffled a boy's hair. "Alright, so what's the plan? What do you all want to do first?"

A chorus of excited voices responded.

"Play cricket!"

"No, football!"

"Bhaiyya, sing us a song first!"

Siva laughed. "One at a time! Alright, let's do this: games first, then songs later.

The group split up into different activities. Imtiaz and Arun got dragged into a cricket match, with Arun dramatically complaining about being made the wicketkeeper. Meenakshi and Anushka helped a few younger kids with drawing and crafts. Ayan, despite not intending to participate much, found himself seated with a few kids, watching as they proudly showed him their sketches.

One little boy, around seven, tugged at Ayan's sleeve. "Bhaiyya, will you help me draw a tiger?"

Ayan hesitated for a moment before nodding. "Alright, let's give it a shot." He took the pencil and carefully started sketching, the boy watching him in awe.

From a distance, Siva observed the scene with a small, knowing smile. He had hoped bringing Ayan here would calm him, even if just for a little while.

As the day continued, they cooked together. The kids ran around, giggling as Siva and Imtiaz tried (and failed) to properly roll out rotis under the supervision of the orphanage's cook. Anushka and Meenakshi handled the vegetables while Arun was on dish duty, grumbling about how unfair his task was.

Siva, holding a ladle, turned dramatically to Anushka. "Do I look like a master chef?"

Anushka smirked. "More like a disaster chef."

The kids burst into laughter as Siva clutched his heart in mock pain. "Betrayed. Right in front of my fans."

Ayan, quietly cutting vegetables, let out a small chuckle; something Siva didn't miss.

After lunch, the children settled down in a circle, and Siva pulled out his guitar.

"Okay, one song, and then storytime," he announced.

The kids cheered as he strummed the first notes, his voice smooth and full of warmth as he sang a soft, familiar tune. The others listened in silence, the melody weaving through the air like a gentle embrace. Anushka watched him, her eyes softening as she rested her chin on her hand.

As the last note faded, the children clapped excitedly. "One more, Bhaiyya!"

Siva chuckled. "Later, promise."

A little girl climbed onto his lap, resting her head against his chest. "Okay... but only because it's your birthday."

His heart melted. "That's fair."

As the sun dipped below the horizon, the orphanage staff gathered everyone in the main hall. Siva thought they were simply winding down, but the moment he stepped inside, the lights dimmed slightly, and the children all yelled in unison...

"HAPPY BIRTHDAY, BHAIYYA!"

Siva blinked in surprise, his eyes widening as he looked around. In the center was a small cake, surrounded by handmade decorations. The kids had made paper flowers, banners, and even small cut-out stars with wishes written on them.

One by one, they handed him tiny handcrafted gifts: woven bracelets, paper crowns, drawings of him playing guitar, and small letters.

A little boy handed him a folded piece of paper. "I wrote this for you, Bhaiyya. You have to read it later, okay?"

Siva crouched, placing a hand on the boy's shoulder. "I promise I will."

As he looked around, taking in the sight of the kids' bright smiles, his friends' warm expressions, and the love surrounding him, his throat tightened with emotion.

Anushka nudged him, whispering. "You're not allowed to cry."

He laughed softly. "Not crying. Just... I don't know. This means a lot."

Ayan, standing slightly apart, watched silently with a genuine, small smile on his face.

"Well, what are you waiting for? Blow out the candles!" Meenakshi urged.

Siva smiled, closed his eyes for a brief moment, and made his wish before blowing out the candles. The room erupted into cheers as he cut the cake, feeding the first bite to the kids before handing slices to everyone.

As laughter and joy filled the night, Siva looked around at the people he loved, feeling something deep and unshakable settle in his heart.

It was the perfect day. And for Ayan, for the first time in a long while, it felt like he wasn't alone. Like, just maybe, he was part of a family.

SEVENTEEN
THE WHITE VIPER

Somewhere far away, deep in the shadowed forests of Pakistan, another kind of gathering was taking place: one not built on joy, but on suspicion, fear, and silent, unspoken threats.

The dim glow of kerosene lamps flickered against the worn-out fabric of the tent, casting long, wavering shadows over the men gathered inside. The air was thick with tension, the scent of damp earth and gun oil clinging to every surface.

Seated at the center of the tent was Ibrahim. To his left stood Kabir, his expression calm as always, his posture straight and composed. And to his right, someone new.

A man, tall and lean, with a shaved face and deep scars running across his forearm, stood with his hands behind his back. His presence was unnerving, his sharp, piercing gaze observing the men seated before him as though he were deciding which of them deserved to breathe another day.

Ibrahim's voice cut through the silence.

"I believe introductions are in order." He gestured to the man beside him. "This is Amar. But to those who know him well, he is the White Viper."

A heavy silence followed. The name alone sent a chill down the spines of the three Indian collaborators seated across from Ibrahim.

They had heard the rumor: whispers of a man who operated in the shadows, a man who dealt in blood and weapons without hesitation. Unlike Kabir, who was known for his calculated methods, Amar was a psychopath, unpredictable, ruthless, a force of destruction with no remorse.

Stephen Davis, the businessman who had long laundered money for the organization, swallowed hard. He had spent years making deals with criminals, but something about this man unsettled him. Beside him sat Suresh Krishna, the leader of India's opposition party, seated uncomfortably in his seat, wiping sweat off his brow. Karim Mohammed, the Mumbai underworld boss, tapped his fingers on the table, his usual arrogance dimmed.

After a long pause, Stephen finally spoke, choosing his words carefully. "We... we have risked everything working with you, Ibrahim. But the recent failures..." He hesitated before adding, "They have shaken our position."

Ibrahim said nothing, merely watching him.

"The authorities are watching," Karim said, his voice low, almost cautious. "The cracks are showing."

Suresh Krishna, despite being a powerful man in Indian politics, was the most visibly shaken. His fingers fumbled as he adjusted his glasses. "We were promised control, but what we see is chaos." He cleared his throat. "If this continues, we might have no choice but to..."

A sharp metallic click echoed through the tent.

Amar had placed a revolver on the table, his fingers lightly tapping the barrel. His lips curled into a smile, but there was no warmth in it.

"Whoever has doubts in their head," he said, his voice smooth yet venomous, "gets a bullet right there, to have clarity." He tapped his forehead with a finger, his grin widening.

No one spoke.

Amar leaned forward, his voice barely above a whisper. "We don't tolerate weakness." His eyes flicked toward Suresh Krishna. "Least of all from men who built their power on our backs."

Suresh stiffened.

Ibrahim finally spoke, his voice calm but carrying the weight of a man whose words dictated life and death. "Failures are merely setbacks. But I do not allow setbacks for too long." His gaze lingered on Stephen, Suresh, and Karim. "Doubt is a disease. It spreads if left unchecked."

Amar chuckled, resting his hand on the revolver. "I'd be happy to check it for you."

Kabir, who had remained silent all this time, finally glanced at Amar, his face Incomprehensible. He had known this was coming. Amar had always been like this: reckless, unpredictable. Where Kabir's strength was in his discipline and focus, Amar thrived on chaos and fear. It was no secret that Amar despised him.

Not because of their differences, but because of Ibrahim's favoritism.

Amar had been with Ibrahim for nearly twenty years, taken in as a war orphan after his parents were killed by the Indian army. His father had been a loyal soldier to Ibrahim, and Amar had witnessed his execution firsthand. His mother had tried to fight back, only to be gunned down in front of him. From that day, Amar had lived for one purpose...to see India burn.

Ibrahim had trained him, shaped him into a lethal weapon. But no matter how much blood Amar spilled, no matter how much he proved himself, Ibrahim's eyes always settled on Kabir. Kabir, the prodigy. Kabir, the future leader.

It enraged Amar.

And Kabir knew it.

But he never reacted. Never rose to Amar's provocations. To Kabir, Amar was a rabid dog: dangerous, but ultimately beneath him.

Ibrahim finally turned back to the seated men. "Your concerns have been heard. And I have already ensured that faith in our strength will not waver." He gestured toward Amar. "From this moment forward, Amar will personally oversee the next phase of our operation."

Amar grinned, his fingers sliding away from the revolver. "Consider it a guarantee."

The tension in the room remained thick, but the message was clear: this was not a negotiation. This was an ultimatum.

Amar and Kabir stepped out as Ibrahim and the partners continued their discussion. It was clear now: whatever was being spoken inside was not meant for them.

Kabir emerged first, stepping into the crisp mountain air, his hands tucked in his pockets. The cold wind howled through the valley, rustling the canvas of the tents, but he barely noticed. His mind was elsewhere. Thinking. Calculating.

A voice, edged with mockery, broke the silence.

"Kabir."

Kabir didn't turn immediately. He exhaled, tilting his head slightly, waiting.

Amar approached from his right, lazily spinning the muzzle of his revolver between his fingers. His movements were effortless, casual, like a man playing with something he had mastered long ago.

"I heard Kabir was all mighty and wise," Amar mused, tilting his head. "The man who does everything with precise calculations." His lips curled into a smirk. "Then tell me, why are all your plans falling apart?"

Kabir said nothing.

Amar took a step closer, his voice thick with amusement. "Maybe everyone overestimated you." He let the revolver spin once more before catching it. "You're nothing special."

His words hung in the cold air between them.

With a final glance, Amar turned away, his tone shifting to something more self-assured. "Now that I'm here, I'll make sure everything is done right."

He took a step forward. Then another.

Just as he was about to disappear into the shadows, Kabir finally spoke. His voice was calm, quiet, yet it carried weight, forcing Amar to stop mid-step.

"Is that right?"

Amar didn't turn, but his grip on the revolver tightened slightly.

"And what exactly are you going to do?" Kabir asked, his tone devoid of mockery, just a simple question that cut deeper because of it.

A short silence followed before Amar scoffed. "Wait and watch."

Kabir exhaled, shaking his head slightly. His voice, still measured, carried the wisdom of someone who had seen far more than he let on.

"A man who underestimates his enemies..." he said, letting the words settle, "does not live long enough to regret it."

Amar stopped again, this time turning his head. The smirk was gone.

"I do not fear the Indian army," he said, his voice steady, his eyes burning with something darker, something personal. "I despise them." A pause. "And I will be the end of them."

Without another word, he walked away, his silhouette vanishing into the night.

Kabir remained where he was, unmoving. His gaze lingered on Amar's retreating figure, but his expression betrayed nothing.

He simply observed.

The meeting had ended. One by one, the partners departed in separate vehicles, their expressions tense with lingering unease. Only Karim remained.

A few minutes after the others left, Ibrahim stepped out of the tent. He glanced at Karim before turning his attention to Amar. "Walk him out," Ibrahim said with a firm tone, before retreating to his tent without another word.

Amar gave a small nod and gestured for Karim to follow. The two walked toward a waiting jeep, their steps slow, deliberate. The atmosphere between them was thick with tension, words hanging between them unspoken.

They stopped near the vehicle, standing close but rigid, exchanging low words that carried the weight of secrecy. Karim's jaw tightened as he listened, his fingers tapping against the metal of the door in thought. A moment passed, heavy and measured, before he finally gave a slow nod.

"It will be done," Karim said, his voice leaving no room for doubt.

Amar didn't react beyond a slight shift in his stance. Without another word, Karim climbed into the back of the jeep. His men blindfolded him and shut the door behind him, and within seconds, the vehicle pulled away, kicking up a trail of dust as it disappeared into the darkness.

Amar stood there for a moment, watching until the red taillights faded. Then, with a slow breath, he turned on his heel and walked back toward the camp.

The next morning, far away from the mountains, the heat of Mumbai wrapped around the city like a thick blanket. Unlike the cold, tense air of the camp, life here moved fast, indifferent to the battles fought elsewhere.

Inside a dimly lit gym, the rhythmic sound of fists slamming against a punching bag filled the space. Ayan, drenched in sweat, moved with precision; each strike controlled, each motion calculated. His muscles tensed with every punch, his breathing steady despite the intensity.

In the corner, Siva sat on a bench, lazily spinning a water bottle in his hands, his phone pressed to his ear. "Yeah, yeah, Anu, I got it. No, I'm not doing anything reckless... for now." His eyes flicked to Ayan, who was entirely focused on the bag. "No, he's just... He smirked. "Being Ayan."

Ayan didn't acknowledge him. He just kept moving: jab, cross, hook, elbow. The force behind each strike made the heavy bag shudder, the chain above creaking from the impact.

Siva shook his head, switching the phone to his other ear. "Yeah, I'll talk to you later... Love you too," He ended the call and leaned back, watching Ayan for a moment before finally speaking.

"You planning to murder that bag, or are you actually gonna take a break?"

Ayan delivered one last powerful strike before stepping back, breathing hard. He grabbed a bottle from the floor, taking a long drink before running a hand through his damp hair. "There are no shortcuts to becoming stronger."

Siva smirked. "Yeah, yeah, keep going at this rate, and you'll collapse. Then I'll have to give you CPR, though I'd really rather not."

Ayan exhaled, rolling his shoulders. "I don't have time to take it slow, Siva. I have to get into the Indian Army. If I want to make it, I need to be better. Stronger."

Siva tossed him a towel. "Well, whatever you do, just don't turn into one of those drill sergeant types who yell at people for breathing wrong."

Ayan smirked slightly but didn't say anything. He wiped his face with the towel, his mind already racing with the next step.

Siva sighed, standing up. "Alright, come on, man. You need actual food if you wanna survive this training obsession of yours."

Without another word, they grabbed their things and headed out. The gym door swung shut behind them.

As Ayan and Siva crossed the college gates on their bikes, the usual buzz of campus life surrounded them: friends chatting, students rushing to classes, and the occasional honk from cars trying to navigate through the crowd. They parked in their usual spot, the engines cutting off as they stepped off.

Siva stretched his arms, letting out a long yawn. "Man, watching you train all morning drained my energy."

Ayan shot him a look as he locked his bike. "You were sitting the whole time."

"Exactly. Do you know how exhausting it is to do nothing?" Siva grinned.

Ayan shook his head, ignoring him as they made their way to the library steps where their friends were gathered.

Arun and Imtiaz were mid-argument, voices raised. Meenakshi sat cross-legged, watching with mild amusement.

"Finally," Arun called out as Ayan and Siva approached. "How was the hardcore training session?"

Siva sighed dramatically. "Brutal. I suffered."

"You suffered?" Meenakshi raised a brow.

"Yes. Mentally. Watching Ayan murder a punching bag for an hour made me feel physically unfit."

The group chuckled, but before the conversation could continue, Siva's eyes flickered toward a bench a little farther away.

Anushka was already there, sitting alone, staring at nothing in particular.

Her shoulders were tense, her usual energy missing.

Siva didn't say a word. He simply walked toward her.

The group exchanged glances. Ayan leaned against the railing, arms crossed, watching.

Siva approached Anushka and placed a hand on her shoulder. She didn't react at first, but after a moment, she turned slightly.

Without a word, Siva sat beside her.

The group remained quiet, observing from a distance.

Arun frowned. "What's up with her?"

Imtiaz smirked. "Maybe Siva did something."

Meenakshi shot him a glare. "Shut up, yaar. It's her family. Something's wrong."

Arun leaned in. "Like what?"

Meenakshi sighed, lowering her voice. "Her dad's been getting threats. You know about his hospital project, right?"

"Yeah," Arun nodded. "The one that's supposed to offer cheap medical care?"

"Exactly. And obviously, the big corporate hospitals don't like that. They see him as a threat to their business. So, there's been pressure...serious pressure."

Arun raised a brow. "That bad?"

Meenakshi nodded. "She didn't say much, but apparently, he didn't even want her to come to college today. They argued, and... he slapped her."

Arun's expression darkened. "What the hell?"

Meenakshi sighed. "She didn't want to talk about it much. Just said that things at home have been really bad. But she still came, though. But you can tell it messed her up."

They glanced toward Anushka and Siva. She was staring at the ground, wiping at her face every few seconds. Siva sat close, speaking softly, his presence steady. He said something that made her let out a weak chuckle.

Ayan exhaled silently, still watching.

A few minutes later, Anushka wiped her eyes and nodded at something Siva said. He stood up first, offering a hand. She took it, letting him pull her up.

As they returned to the group, Anushka forced a small smile. "Okay, can we stop looking at me like I'm some tragic story?"

Arun raised his hands in surrender. "Hey, no judgment. Just making sure you're good."

Anushka exhaled. "I will be."

Siva clapped his hands together. "Alright, now that my counseling session is over, who's buying me lunch?"

Imtiaz scoffed. "Keep dreaming."

The group laughed, the tension lifting slightly. Anushka still seemed distant, but she tried. No one knew that, in the background, a plan was already in motion.

Later that evening..

The grand halls of the Singhania mansion were quieter than usual, save for the faint ticking of the antique clock in the living room. The air was thick, not with warmth, but with something heavier, an unspoken tension that had been lingering for weeks.

Anushka sat curled up on the far end of the couch, absently scrolling through her phone. She wasn't paying attention to the screen, though. Her mind was elsewhere: on her father, on the sharp tone in his voice lately, on the way her mother had been quieter than usual.

Across the room, she heard the faint creak of the study door opening. Footsteps...her father's. Then her mother's voice, low but firm.

"Rajveer, you can't keep this from her forever."

Anushka stiffened, her finger hovering over her phone screen. She had never heard her mother sound so... worried.

"She doesn't need to know," her father responded, his voice calmer but heavy. "I won't let her live in fear."

Her mother's sigh followed. "But the threats, Rajveer. This isn't just business rivalry. Stephen Davis…"

Anushka frowned. Stephen Davis?

Her father cut in, his voice sharper this time. "I don't care about Stephen. I've dealt with people like him before. Let them do what they want. This hospital is happening, and nothing will stop me."

A silence followed. Anushka leaned in slightly, trying to hear more, but then her mother's footsteps. The study door closed again.

She exhaled, leaning back into the couch, her heart beating a little faster. Stephen Davis. Her father had sounded angry. And her mother… she sounded scared.

What was really going on?

The next day, the group had already gathered at their usual spot when Anushka arrived late. She walked toward them, her bag slung over one shoulder, looking slightly uneasy.

Siva noticed first. "You're late," he said, leaning back against his bike. "That's rare."

Anushka sighed, brushing her hair out of her face. "My driver took a different route today."

Arun raised a brow. "Why?"

She hesitated for a moment before answering. "I think… someone was following us."

That got their attention. Meenakshi straightened, her expression sharpening. "What do you mean?"

Anushka exhaled. "I noticed a black SUV behind us. It stayed in our lane for a while, even when we switched roads. I thought it was just a coincidence, but the moment I really started paying attention, it disappeared." She shook her head. "I don't know, maybe I'm just overthinking it, but it felt… off."

Siva and Ayan exchanged a quick glance.

"Probably nothing," Ayan said, keeping his tone casual. "Maybe just another car taking the same route."

Anushka gave a small nod, though she still looked uncertain. "Yeah, maybe."

Siva nudged her lightly. "You're overthinking, Anu. But if it makes you feel better, we'll keep an eye out."

That seemed to ease her nerves a little. The group chatted for a bit longer before heading to class.

Once they were inside, Siva leaned toward Ayan and spoke in a low voice. "This looks shady."

Ayan's jaw tightened. "Agreed. It'd be better if she stayed home for a while. Exams are coming up anyway, and she could use the time to study."

Siva nodded. "Good excuse. I'll try to convince her."

Neither of them said it out loud, but they both knew this wasn't something to ignore.

A few days passed, and Anushka decided to stay home, not just because Siva had asked her to, but because her father had become unusually persistent. It wasn't like she had much of a choice.

Meanwhile, Ayan and Siva had done a little digging into the black car she'd mentioned. They asked around, checked for any signs of suspicious activity, but found nothing solid. Maybe it really was nothing. Or maybe whoever was behind it had just gone quiet. Either way, there was no point in overthinking it, at least for now.

Siva made it a habit to check in on Anushka regularly, either through calls or sneaky late-night visits to her house. How he managed to get past all the security was anyone's guess, but knowing Anushka, she probably had something to do with it.

Days turned into weeks, and soon enough, their second-year final exams were upon them.

Everyone tackled the exams with their usual mix of stress, caffeine, and last-minute cramming. Ayan was as focused as ever, Meenakshi and Imtiaz studied like their lives depended on it, and even Arun pulled off decent scores. Anushka, despite missing classes, aced most of her subjects.

And then there was Siva.

When results day arrived, he stood staring at his mark sheet like it had personally betrayed him. Three red marks. Three subjects failed.

Imtiaz peeked over his shoulder and let out a low whistle. "Oof. Tough break, buddy."

Arun clapped Siva on the back with a grin. "Maybe if you had focused a little more on your books and a little less on Anushka, you wouldn't be in this mess."

Siva groaned. "Oh, shut up, yaar."

Anushka, who had been silent until now, crossed her arms and narrowed her eyes at him. "Three subjects, Siva?"

Siva gulped. "...Yeah?"

She shook her head. "Unbelievable."

"I mean, in my defense..."

"No excuses." She pointed a finger at him. "I am not speaking to you until you pass."

Siva's eyes widened. "Wait, what?"

Anushka turned on her heel and walked away.

Siva looked at the others for help. Meenakshi simply smirked. Imtiaz shrugged. Arun? He was already laughing.

Ayan clapped Siva's shoulder. "Good luck, idiot."

And just like that, Siva found himself facing his biggest challenge yet: not the exams, not even his failure... but Anushka's cold shoulder.

EIGHTEEN
A MOMENT'S PAUSE

For days, Anushka had refused to talk to Siva. Ever since the results had come out and he'd failed his exams, she'd been furious. She had warned him to focus, reminded him over and over again, and still, he had messed up.

So, she did what she had threatened. She ignored him.

But Siva wasn't the type to give up easily.

After multiple failed attempts to get her attention, he finally convinced her to meet him at a café in the mall. It took relentless persuasion, a few texted apologies, and the promise that he was genuinely studying. She agreed, but only because she had cooled off a little, and deep down, she missed him.

Somehow, Siva also managed to drag Ayan along.

Ayan had refused at first, uninterested in their childish arguments. But eventually, he agreed, mostly because the public library was right across the street.. He figured he might as well pick up a few books while they were there.

"Fine," Ayan had said, rolling his eyes. "But don't expect me to play mediator between you two."

And so, the plan was set.

The mall was alive with weekend energy: shoppers chatting, families strolling, the scent of coffee and baked goods drifting through the air. Near the café entrance, Siva stood tapping his phone, checking the time, knowing Anushka would arrive any minute.

When she finally did, his face lit up.

But she didn't smile back.

She barely looked at him, her expression distant, her arms crossed. Instead, she turned toward Ayan, offering him a much warmer greeting.

"Hey, Ayan. How've you been?"

Ayan shrugged. "Same old. You?"

"Nothing much," she sighed, shaking her head.

Siva cleared his throat, forcing a grin. "Wow, so I don't even exist now? This is new."

Anushka shot him a sharp glance but said nothing.

Undeterred, Siva pressed on. "Look, I know I messed up. But I've been studying. I swear. Ask Ayan."

Ayan raised an eyebrow. "I mean, I've never seen him study before, but... lately, that's all he's been doing."

Anushka's expression softened. Just a little. A hint of a smile tugged at the corner of her lips.

"Well... that's good, I guess."

Siva grinned, relieved that the ice was starting to crack. "See? Told you."

Ayan, sensing his job was done, turned toward the exit. "You two go inside. I'll meet you later."

Anushka frowned. "Wait, you're not joining us? You can't just leave me alone with this guy."

"I've got books to pick up," Ayan said. "I'll be back in an hour."

And with that, he walked off.

The library was quiet. Ayan wandered the aisles, scanning the spines of old, familiar titles. But he couldn't shake the nagging unease in the back of his mind.

Something felt off.

Then...

A distant, deafening boom.

The ground trembled beneath him. A split second later, a shockwave rocked the building. Books tumbled from the shelves, and people screamed. Ayan's heart slammed against his ribs as he turned toward the entrance, his pulse roaring in his ears.

Smoke.

Thick, black smoke.

His legs moved before his mind could catch up, carrying him out of the library, across the street, toward the chaos...

Toward the mall.

People were screaming, running in every direction. Cars swerved, bikes roared past, and horns blared. But Ayan kept moving, blind to the mayhem, or unwilling to care.. A car screeched to a halt inches from him as he stepped onto the road, but he didn't flinch.

What had been a bustling center of life moments ago was now a mangled heap of steel, glass, and fire. People screamed. Sirens wailed. Dust and debris choked the air.

Ayan pushed through the crowd, shoving past frantic onlookers, his eyes locked on one place...the café.

Or what was left of it.

His breath caught.

No.

The café was gone. Just rubble. Scorched, broken, unrecognizable.

Ayan stared at the rubble, and in that moment, he knew, Siva and Anushka were dead.

Ayan's knees nearly buckled. His hands curled into fists, nails digging into his palms. He staggered forward, searching, desperate, refusing to believe what his eyes were telling him.

"Siva!"

No answer.

"Anushka!"

Silence.

Just a gaping hole where they had been.

His vision blurred. His breath came in short, ragged bursts. Somewhere in the chaos, people were yelling, first responders rushing to the scene, but Ayan heard none of it.

Because they were gone.

Hours passed.

Ayan sat on the curb, motionless. His hands were scraped, covered in dried blood from clawing through the wreckage. His face was blank, empty. The fire had long been put out, but the smoke still lingered, curling into the darkening sky.

Raghav arrived, pushing through the crowd. When he found Ayan, he knelt beside him, placing a firm hand on his shoulder.

Ayan didn't move.

Didn't speak.

Raghav helped Ayan to the car, his grip firm but gentle. He knew that letting Ayan stay at the scene any longer would only deepen the damage. Without a word, he guided him into the passenger seat and began the drive home.

Silence filled the car. Ayan sat staring out the window, eyes fixed on nothing, the world outside blurring past like it no longer mattered. Raghav gripped the wheel, saying nothing, because there was nothing left to say.

He went to his room without a word. He sat on the bed, staring at the floor, his hands resting on his lap.

He didn't cry.

Didn't scream.

Didn't feel anything at all.

Raghav lingered in the doorway, watching him, the weight of helplessness pressing down on him like a stone. He wanted to say something, but what words could fix this?

So he left him alone.

Ayan stayed there for hours, unmoving.

Thinking of nothing.

Hearing nothing.

Except for the explosion, replaying in his mind.

"Ayan," Raghav said softly, "I'll be in the hall if you need anything."

But Ayan didn't respond.

Raghav stood for a moment longer, staring at him, before turning to leave the room. He knew there was no use trying to comfort Ayan. The boy was beyond reach.

Sitting down in one of the chairs, he took a deep breath, trying to steady himself. The chaos of the day still lingered in his mind, and for a moment, he allowed himself to be consumed by the weight of it all. But he couldn't let himself break down. Not now. Not when everything depended on staying composed.

Raghav picked up his phone and dialed a number, only one person on his mind: the people still handling the investigation. Despite his retirement, Raghav's name still carried weight. Even though he was no longer an active officer, he had once been the head of the operation focused on dealing with terrorist threats. The contacts he had made over the years remained loyal, and whenever something urgent arose, they didn't hesitate to reach out to him.

The phone rang once, twice, before a familiar voice answered.

"Raghav," came the voice from the other end, calm but with an undercurrent of urgency. "I was about to call you. We need you at the Army gathering point. We're going over the details of the blast. There are a few things we need to discuss."

"I'll be there," he replied with a sharp tone.

He hung up the phone and leaned back in the chair for a moment, his mind racing. He couldn't afford to get lost in his emotions. Not now, not when things were just beginning to unravel. He stood up, his body stiff from the weight of everything that had happened, and made his way to the door.

Before leaving, he glanced toward Ayan's room, his heart aching. He couldn't imagine that Ayan had to go through this again: losing people he loved, feeling that crushing sense of helplessness. But he knew Ayan needed him now more than ever. Still, Raghav couldn't allow himself to be consumed by it. There were things to be done, answers to be found.

Once Raghav entered the meeting room, the air felt heavy with unspoken questions and anticipation. The officers present sat in tense silence, their expressions grim. Raghav took his seat, his mind still clouded with the image of Ayan sitting motionless in his room.

"The blast radius suggests high-grade explosives," one officer reported. "Professionally set. This wasn't random. It was an act of terrorism."

Raghav's jaw clenched.

"We've been combing through the debris," another officer said. "There wasn't much left intact, but..." He hesitated.

Then he placed something on the table.

A small object.

A figurine.

White.

Coiled.

A viper.

Silence strangled the room. No one spoke. No one needed to.

Because they all knew what it meant.

Who it meant.

The White Viper.

And that meant one thing:

This was just the beginning.

For days, Ayan stayed inside his room.

He didn't eat much.

Didn't sleep much.

Didn't speak at all.

He just existed.

He thought grief would feel different this time. That he had changed. That he had learned how to live with loss.

But he hadn't.

Siva was gone. Anushka was gone.

And suddenly, it was happening all over again.

The emptiness. The silence. The weight pressing down on his chest, making it hard to breathe.

It felt just like that day.

The day he lost everything.

Now, he was back in the same place, watching the people he cared about disappear.

And there was nothing he could do about it.

But today, he had to step out.

Because today, he had to say goodbye.

He grabbed his jacket, stepped out of his room, and left without a word.

The roads blurred past as he rode, the world outside moving too fast, too loud, while everything inside him remained painfully still.

And then, he was there.

Anushka's house was crowded.

Too many people.

Businessmen, politicians, professors: faces he had never seen before. People who barely knew her, but had shown up because of her last name.

Outside, reporters whispered behind their cameras, turning her death into just another breaking news story.

Ayan ignored them and walked in.

The air was thick with grief.

Meenakshi was on the floor, her arms wrapped around the empty casket, sobbing in a way that made others look away. Not the kind of crying that could be comforted. The kind that ripped through the soul.

Imtiaz and Arun sat beside her, trying to be strong, but their own faces were broken. Their hands trembled as they held onto each other, as if letting go would make it all feel real.

Ayan watched from a distance.

Not because he didn't care. But because he didn't know how to grieve.

He wasn't sure he even remembered how.

"Goodbye, Anushka," he whispered. "You were a good person. This shouldn't have happened."

Then he turned to leave.

Not because he wanted to.

But because he didn't know what else to do..

Ayan was almost out the door when something caught his eye.

A black SUV.

It was parked too close to the entrance, its tinted windows giving it an air of suspicion.

Ayan's feet moved on their own, drawing him closer to the black SUV. He needed to see more, needed to be sure. His eyes scanned the car, trying to make out any details, but before he could get closer, the engine revved suddenly. The car surged forward, its tires screeching against the pavement as it accelerated sharply.

Ayan froze for a split second, then rushed toward the front gate, heart pounding in his chest. But it was too late. The SUV was already speeding down the road, its rear lights disappearing around the corner.

A wave of frustration crashed over him. He had been too slow. Too hesitant.

He stood there for a moment, staring at the empty road, the engine's hum lingering in the air. And then it hit him: a memory, sudden and sharp. He had seen that car before.

The day of the blast.

Ayan's mind scrambled as the pieces fell together. He remembered running toward the mall, fear driving him faster with every step. And then, that black SUV had passed by him, so close it almost hit him. He hadn't thought much of it at the time. People were panicking, trying to escape; he had assumed they were just another group trying to get away.

But now... now, that same car was here. A cold shiver ran down his spine as the memory flickered in his mind, his eyes widening as the connection became clearer.

Anushka's words cut through his thoughts, the ones she had said to him weeks ago: "I think someone's following me. A black SUV."

Ayan's pulse quickened. The car wasn't a coincidence. It couldn't be.

The realization hit him like a punch to the gut. He wasn't sure what it meant yet, but he knew one thing: something was terribly wrong, and he had to find out what it was.

Ayan's heart raced as the realization sank in. He pulled his phone from his pocket with trembling hands and quickly dialed Raghav's number. The line rang, each tone amplifying his growing unease. When Raghav finally answered, Ayan didn't wait for pleasantries.

"Raghav, where are you?" After a brief pause, Ayan continued, "I need to speak with you. I'm coming," his voice tight with urgency.

Ayan barely remembered the ride to Raghav's house. His mind was racing, pieces of a puzzle clicking together faster than he could process. The SUV. The blast. Anushka's fear. It all connected, and now, the one person who could help him make sense of it all was Raghav.

As soon as he stepped inside, he didn't waste a second.

"I need to speak with you," Ayan said, his voice tense.

Raghav, who had been seated in the living room, glanced up. He immediately noticed the shift in Ayan's expression. This wasn't just grief; this was something else. Something urgent.

"Sit down," Raghav said, gesturing to the couch, but Ayan shook his head.

"A few weeks ago, before the blast," Ayan began, his voice steady but strained, "Anushka mentioned something... a black SUV following her."

Raghav leaned forward, his brows furrowing.

"Following her?"

Ayan nodded. "Me and Siva... His voice faltered at Siva's name, but he swallowed the pain and continued. "We checked, but we didn't find anything. Thought maybe she was imagining it. She was upset that day. And... she also said her dad was getting threats. From other businessmen."

Raghav listened intently, but his expression barely changed, until Ayan mentioned the name.

"Especially from a man called Stephen Davis."

Raghav's head snapped up. His eyes sharpened with sudden recognition.

"Stephen Davis?" He repeated, his tone shifting. "You mean the business tycoon?"

"Yes," Ayan confirmed. "Apparently, he was one of the people threatening her father."

Raghav exhaled, rubbing his chin as if piecing something together. "I see... I wonder what that was about."

Ayan clenched his fists. "That's not all."

Raghav's gaze locked onto Ayan's. "Then what?"

Ayan hesitated. He wasn't sure why, but suddenly, saying it out loud made everything feel more real, more terrifying. He took a slow breath.

"That day... the blast."

Raghav stiffened.

"I was running towards the mall," Ayan continued, his voice quieter now. "And suddenly, a black SUV sped past me. It was so fast, so close, it almost hit me."

Raghav's expression hardened. "The same one?"

"I didn't think about it at the time," Ayan admitted. "Didn't care. There were so many people running for their lives, it didn't seem important. But today... at Anushka's funeral..." He exhaled sharply. "That same SUV was parked outside her house."

Raghav's jaw tightened.

"It was like they were watching," Ayan said, his voice lower now. "I tried to approach, but the moment I did, they took off. It was like they knew I saw them. And that's when it all came together..."

Silence hung in the room. Raghav was staring at the floor, his mind visibly working through Ayan's words. Then, suddenly, his eyes widened, like something had just clicked into place.

"I see..." he muttered, mostly to himself. "Now it all makes more sense."

Ayan's stomach twisted. "What makes sense?"

Raghav's gaze lifted, serious and tensed.

"You better prepare for this."

Ayan froze, the words hanging heavy in the air. There was something final in Raghav's tone...something that made his stomach clench.

Raghav took a breath before he spoke. "We know who's behind the attack," he said. "But we didn't know why." His eyes met Ayan's. "Now, I think I have a theory."

Ayan's hands curled into fists. He didn't need to hear more. His voice was tight with anger when he asked, "It was him, wasn't it?"

Raghav didn't answer immediately.

"Kabir," Ayan spat the name like venom.

But Raghav shook his head. "No. It wasn't Kabir."

Ayan blinked. "What?"

Raghav leaned forward. "At the blast site, our team found something. A small sculpture."

Ayan frowned. "A sculpture?"

Raghav nodded. "A White Viper."

A chill ran down Ayan's spine. "White Viper?"

Raghav's expression darkened. "It's a signature. A calling card." His voice was grim. "White Viper is one of the most notorious criminals in the world. Wherever he goes, chaos and death follow. And every time, he leaves one thing behind."

Ayan already knew the answer. His throat felt dry as he whispered, "The White Viper."

Raghav nodded.

"He's a ghost," Raghav continued. "Untouchable. Infamous. Governments fear him. Law enforcement across the world has tried to track him down, but he always vanishes. No one knows what he looks like, only the destruction he leaves behind."

Ayan clenched his jaw, trying to understand what this meant.

"That's not all," Raghav said. His voice was lower now, more intense. "The White Viper doesn't work alone. He works for an organization. One led by none other than..."

He paused, looking at Ayan carefully before saying the name.

"Ibrahim Al Malik."

Ayan's body went rigid. His breath hitched.

The name itself was enough to send a cold shiver down him. He had heard it before. The world had. Ibrahim Al Malik was a name spoken in hushed voices, a name that carried fear, destruction, and death.

Raghav watched as Ayan absorbed the information.

"Ibrahim," Ayan muttered. His chest tightened. "He was behind this?"

Raghav nodded. "We didn't know why a terrorist of his level would focus on a shopping mall in Mumbai. It didn't make sense." He leaned back, thinking. "But now, I think I do."

Ayan met his gaze. "Anushka?"

Raghav sighed. "We're not sure yet. But based on what you told me, it sounds like they were tracking her for some time. They probably tapped her phone. That blast..." Raghav exhaled. "It wasn't random. It was targeted. And somehow, I feel it was a message. Or a warning. For her father."

Ayan felt sick.

Anushka wasn't just collateral damage.

She was the target.

"This is too much," Ayan murmured, shaking his head. "I can't... He stopped himself, closing his eyes for a second. He needed to stay in control. "So what do we do now?"

Raghav hesitated. "I have a theory, but I'm not sure. One of Mr. Singhania's enemies may be working with White Viper. Or Ibrahim himself."

Ayan felt his pulse quicken. "Stephen."

Raghav didn't confirm it, but the look in his eyes was enough.

"Then we should arrest him," Ayan said firmly.

But Raghav shook his head.

"We won't be doing anything."

Ayan's eyes widened in shock. "What? Why not?"

"Because," Raghav said, his voice calm but firm, "one, you're a college student. And two...I'm retired."

Ayan clenched his fists.

"And three," Raghav continued, "we have no solid proof. We can't just arrest a man based on assumptions, especially with a terrorism accusation."

Ayan's mind raced for another solution. "What about Mr. Singhania? He could speak against him."

"He just lost his daughter, Ayan. Do you think he'll be talking to anyone for a while?"

Ayan felt a deep frustration settle inside him.

Raghav sighed. "Leave this to me. I'll talk to the right people. I'll make sure this gets looked into."

Ayan swallowed hard, his mind still buzzing. But he knew one thing.

This wasn't over.

Raghav exhaled deeply, rubbing his temples as he stood up. "Give me a minute," he said, heading to his room to change.

Ayan remained on the couch, staring at nothing in particular. His mind was a blur of memories, images flashing one after another.

When Raghav returned, now dressed in fresh clothes, he noticed Ayan still in the same position, lost in thought. He sat down across from him, watching the quiet storm brewing in the boy's eyes.

"I know this is too much," Raghav said finally. "But I know you more than anyone. And I promise you, the ones responsible for Siva and Anushka will pay."

Ayan didn't respond, but his jaw clenched, and his hands curled into fists. There was no grief in his eyes. Only cold, simmering rage. It sent a chill through Raghav. He had seen that look before. He had seen it in men who had nothing left to lose.

The silence was interrupted by Ayan's phone ringing. He glanced at the screen. Arun.

Without hesitation, he declined the call and tossed the phone aside.

Raghav, who had been watching, sighed. "You should speak to them," he said. "They need you as much as you need them right now."

Ayan scoffed. "I don't need anyone." His voice was low but firm. "I know how to be alone. Been doing that since I was seven, remember?"

Raghav flinched at those words. He had no response.

A moment of heavy silence passed between them. Then, after a deep breath, Raghav changed the subject. "Aren't you going to the orphanage?"

Ayan barely spared him a glance. "Why?" he said flatly. "It's not like there's anyone to bury."

Raghav shook his head. "That's not the point of a funeral, Ayan. It's about saying goodbye. It's about closure. It's...

Ayan's face turned red with anger as he stood up abruptly, his chair scraping against the floor.

"I'll say my farewell when I put the bastards responsible six feet underground." His voice was sharp, filled with a chilling resolve.

Raghav opened his mouth to say something, but Ayan had already turned and walked out.

NINETEEN

THE SILENT WAR

The days blurred into each other, an endless cycle of sweat, bruises, and silence. Ayan had locked himself away from the world once again, drowning in a routine that left no room for distractions. He attended college because he had to. He trained because he needed to. He researched because it was the only thing that kept him from spiraling into complete hopelessness.

Arun, Imtiaz, and Meenakshi tried at first. They approached him between classes, attempted casual conversations, and even invited him to join them for tea. Ayan ignored them. He would offer curt nods or a passing glance, but never words. Eventually, they gave up, their voices fading into the background, becoming just another part of the noise he shut out; because the person who once glued them all together was no more.

During the day, he pushed his body to the limit, spending hours in the gym until his muscles screamed in protest. He studied just enough to pass, ensuring he remained on track to graduate. The real work began at night. In the quiet solitude of his room, he pored over every scrap of information he could find on Stephen Davis, the White Viper, and Ibrahim Al Malik. There were too many missing pieces, too many gaps he couldn't fill. But he was patient. He had to be.

His research notes from months ago were scattered, unfocused, driven by pure rage and desperation. Now, as he compared them to his recent findings, he saw a shift: his thoughts were sharper, his deductions clearer. The chaos in his mind had begun to align into a strategy. He was no longer just reacting to his pain; he was planning. Calculating.

Ayan knew the truth: he was powerless. Right now, he was just another college student, weak and insignificant in the grand scheme of things. If he tried to act now, he would be crushed before he even made a dent. So, he made a choice. He would wait. He would finish college. He would join the army. He would become something more than just a survivor.

And when the time comes, he would strike.

For now, the war remained silent, but Ayan was preparing for the day it would begin.

Ayan's persistence eventually led him to Mr. Singhania's doorstep. At first, the man refused to speak, grief and exhaustion etched into his face. Each visit ended in cold silence, in polite yet firm dismissals. But Ayan kept returning, not with demands, not with force, but with presence.

The first few times, Singhania barely acknowledged him. Then, after weeks of quiet persistence, something shifted.

One evening, the weight of everything finally cracked the man's silence.

Singhania exhaled sharply, staring past Ayan as if reliving the nightmare. "I tried everything," he said, voice hollow. "I went to the police, I reached out to officials, anyone who could stop them. But Stephen had his claws in them. Politics, law, the system... all of it bent to his will."

Ayan remained silent, absorbing every word. This wasn't just about power; it was about control. Stephen and the people backing him had influence in places that mattered.

"They didn't want me to go forward with the hospital," Singhania continued. "Not unless I played by their rules. I refused. So they threatened Anushka." His voice wavered. "At first, I thought it was just a bluff: a scare tactic to force me into submission. But then I realized... they don't bluff."

Ayan clenched his fists under the table. "Why did they care about the hospital?"

Singhania let out a bitter chuckle. "Because it was meant to be independent. No under-the-table deals, no influence from their people. Just a place that actually helped the ones who needed it." He scoffed. "That's a threat to people like Stephen. Control means everything to them. If they can't own it, they destroy it."

Ayan felt the weight of those words settle in his mind. This wasn't random violence. Anushka and Siva's deaths weren't just warnings... they were statements.

Stephen had ensured that no one crossed him.

But Ayan wasn't looking to fight Stephen. Not yet. He needed to understand. To connect the pieces. How deep did Stephen's influence go? How far did his connections spread?

And most importantly, how did a businessman like Stephen have enough power to command someone like the White Viper? A brutal terrorist wouldn't move for money alone. There had to be something bigger at play.

This couldn't have been just about a hospital.

Ayan left that night with more questions than answers, but one thing was clear: Stephen wasn't just another corrupt businessman. He was a piece of something much bigger.

And Ayan needed to find out what.

His research continued, and the days kept passing. What started as scattered notes had now become a structured archive: his desk cluttered with documents, his hard drive filled with reports, transaction records, and everything he could find on Stephen Davis. Names of businessmen, politicians, and intermediaries formed a tangled web of influence, but one name stood out above all.

Suresh Krishna.

A sitting Member of Parliament. Leader of the opposition party. A man with enough power to shift policies and silence dissent. And somehow, he was tied to Stephen Davis.

Ayan leaned back in his chair, staring at the name he had highlighted over and over again. This wasn't just about corruption.

This was something bigger: something that dictated who lived and who died.

And he was just a college student.

He had known from the beginning that he had no power, but seeing the scale of influence in front of him made that fact even clearer.

To move forward, he needed power. He needed authority.

Months passed, and Ayan's focus never wavered. He pushed through his final exams with the same discipline he had applied to everything else: efficient, precise, and without distraction. He didn't celebrate when they ended. There was no relief, no sense of freedom. The next phase had already been decided.

One evening, he approached Raghav in his study. The older man glanced up from his files, sensing the weight behind Ayan's silence before he even spoke.

"I want to join the squad," Ayan said, his voice steady.

Raghav leaned back in his chair, studying him. "You've thought this through?"

"There's nothing to think about."

"There's everything to think about," Raghav countered. "If you start this path, there's no turning back. No pause button. Once you wear that uniform, you will be bound by the system, by rules you may not always agree with."

Ayan met his gaze without hesitation. "This is the only way to achieve my purpose."

Raghav sighed, rubbing his temples. "Ayan..."

"This is all I have lived for since I was seven," Ayan's voice was cold, unshaken. "I will hunt the White Viper, drag him out of whatever hole he's hiding in, and make him pay for what he did. Then, I will find Kabir...no matter how long it takes, and I will avenge my family."

Raghav exhaled slowly, searching his face for any trace of doubt. There was none. Ayan's resolve was absolute.

Finally, Raghav nodded. "Then I'll make the arrangements."

With his influence, Raghav made the next steps easy, setting Ayan on the path he had been preparing for all his life. The process was long but necessary. The army recruitment took time, demanding discipline, physical endurance, and unwavering focus. Ayan embraced it, pushing through every challenge with the same determination that had kept him alive all these years. There was no hesitation, no second-guessing. This was the only way forward.

After completing his training, Raghav stepped in once more, securing Ayan a place in the Anti-Terrorist Squad.

His first mission came swiftly, and fate played its hand: their target was none other than the White Viper.

The team was small but precise, each member an expert in their own field. Ayan was the hand-to-hand combat specialist, the one who would get up close and personal. Their sniper, Vikram, a marksman with deadly accuracy, covered them from a distance. Their hacker, Riya, was a genius with technology, breaking through encrypted files and tracking their enemies. Their transportation expert, Mohit, ensured they had a way in and out of any situation, whether it was flying, driving, or navigating through hostile terrain. And finally, their Captain, Karan Mehta, ruthless, strategic, and unshaken, led them toward the hunt.

The war was no longer silent. It had begun.

Karan gathered the team in the briefing room, a large screen displaying intel on their new target.

"The White Viper," Karan began, his voice steady. "A dangerous man working for, or with, Ibrahim. We have reason to believe he was here almost a year ago. And we have strong evidence tying him to the mall bombing ten months back."

Ayan remained silent, but the vein on his forehead pulsed with restrained fury. He exhaled, forcing himself to stay calm.

Karan pointed to the screen, which now displayed an image of a small, intricately carved sculpture: a viper coiled and ready to strike.

"This," Karan continued, "is our proof. It's said that whenever or wherever the White Viper himself attacks, he leaves this behind as his signature. He likes the fame, I guess. But here's the real question: why would someone at his rank be involved in something like a mall bombing? A low-level terrorist could've done that. Why him?"

He paused before adding, "Until recently, we couldn't understand it. But we received new intel."

Everyone leaned in.

"We can't verify this yet, so it stays classified. Except for Ayan... who already knows."

All eyes turned to Ayan, but he kept his gaze fixed on the board.

Karan continued. "Rajveer Singhania, one of the wealthiest businessmen in Mumbai, had plans to establish a hospital offering free medical care to the public. Some people didn't like that. We believe the real target of the blast was his daughter, Anushka Singhania. She was only twenty."

Silence filled the room.

"The significance of this hospital and why someone like the White Viper himself carried out the attack remains unknown," Karan admitted. "It doesn't make sense. Why use a man of his caliber for something like this?"

Ayan spoke at last. His voice was calm, yet the weight behind it was undeniable. "Actually... we do know."

Even Karan looked surprised. "What do you mean?"

Ayan's eyes remained locked on the screen. "I spoke with Mr. Singania. He mentioned that the threats from other businessmen were direct, but a certain someone had threatened his daughter's life specifically. That's what truly scared him."

He exhaled sharply, his fingers tightening into a fist. His next words cut through the room like a blade. "That certain someone was Stephen Davis."

Silence.

Karan's expression darkened, his jaw tightening. Riya's fingers hovered over her keyboard, her usually sharp focus momentarily broken. Vikram leaned forward, his brows furrowed, as if trying to process the weight of the accusation. Mohit let out a low whistle, shaking his head.

"You're telling me," Mohit finally spoke, his voice laced with disbelief, "that Stephen Davis, one of the wealthiest, most influential businessmen in the country, personally threatened Singania's daughter?"

Ayan met his gaze without hesitation. "Yes. And that's just the beginning."

Karan's eyes narrowed. "Go on."

Ayan took a deep breath before continuing. "I've been researching Stephen Davis for months. He is a rich and powerful man, but trust me, he is not what he appears to be. He meets with individuals who don't align with his lifestyle or business, and at odd hours in unusual locations. He's been blackmailing and threatening others, and yet... every complaint against him disappears. Nothing ever gets registered. No action is taken."

Karan frowned. "Because he's rich?"

Ayan's next words dropped like a guillotine. "Not just that." His voice was calm, deliberate, carrying the weight of something irreversible. He let the silence stretch, forcing them to feel it before delivering the final blow.

"Stephen Davis isn't acting alone. He has a lifeline at the very top. A man beyond the reach of law... beyond consequence."

His gaze swept the room, locking onto each of them before he spoke the name that would shatter their perception of power itself.

"Suresh Krishna."

The room didn't just fall silent; it felt like the air had been sucked out entirely.

Karan's brows furrowed as he studied Ayan, his fingers tapping lightly against the table in thought. Vikram, who had barely spoken since the briefing began, exhaled through his nose, his posture stiffening. Riya, who had been observing quietly until now, straightened in her seat, her eyes narrowing.

Vikram let out a low whistle. "You're telling me Suresh Krishna, the man tipped to be the next Prime Minister, is mixed up in this?"

Ayan didn't blink. "Not mixed up. Probably in control."

A hush followed, thick and suffocating. It was one thing to suspect corruption, another to hear a name so powerful spoken in the same breath as terrorism.

Karan leaned forward, his voice even but firm. "You better have proof."

Ayan met his gaze, unwavering. "I don't make accusations. I make cases."

Ayan's eyes didn't waver. "I have proof to back up everything I just said." He let the weight of those words settle before continuing. "Now, what I'm about to say next…is an assumption. But it's based on strong information I've gathered."

The room was deathly silent.

Ayan leaned forward slightly, his voice steady. "Mumbai. Delhi. Kashmir. We've seen countless terrorist activities in recent years. Yes, we've stopped many. But they keep happening. Why? How?" His gaze swept across the room. "How do terrorists like the White Viper and Kabir enter and exit the country as they please?"

He let the question linger before delivering the answer.

"Suresh Krishna."

The air turned heavy.

Karan's fingers twitched. Riya's lips parted, but no words came out. Even Karan's usual composure faltered for a split second.

Ayan didn't stop. "It's all for him to reach the top."

A cold realization settled over them.

"Just imagine, wave after wave of terrorist attacks while the current PM struggles to maintain control. Too much pressure, too much chaos, and when the elections come…" Ayan exhaled sharply. "The people lose faith in the ruling party. And who is next in line for Prime Minister?"

Riya barely whispered, "Suresh Krishna…"

A muscle ticked in Karan's jaw. His voice was quieter this time, but sharper. "Then what's Stephen's role in this?"

Before Ayan could respond, another voice cut in.

"Money."

All eyes turned to Mohit, who had been silent until now. He leaned back, arms crossed, but his gaze was locked onto Ayan.

Ayan gave a small nod. "Exactly." His voice was firm. "Stephen is the one funding these missions. And if my guess is right, there's at least one or two more people involved: operatives working at the base level, handling travel, accommodations, ensuring smooth execution."

The weight of his words pressed down on the room. No one spoke, but the unspoken realization was clear.

This wasn't just corruption.

This was treason.

The room was silent. Even the captain hadn't expected the meeting to take this turn.

Karan finally exhaled, breaking the heavy stillness. "How do we even move in on someone like Suresh?"

No one had an answer.

Without wasting time, Karan stood. "Ayan, come with me."

They left the room together, heading to report their findings to Karan's higher-ups. The others remained seated, exchanging glances as the weight of the information sank in. This wasn't just another operation. This was bigger, more dangerous than any of them had imagined.

Hours passed, stretching into an uneasy silence.

When Karan and Ayan returned, their expressions were unreadable. But there was no hesitation in Karan's voice as he addressed the team.

"Alright team, here's what we're going to do." His tone was firm, decisive. "I'll be straight with you. We can't go after Suresh Krishna. Not yet."

No one looked surprised, but the frustration was evident.

Karan continued, "Which means our next move is Stephen Davis. We bring him down, and we make sure we get enough evidence to drag Suresh Krishna down with him."

He turned to Riya. "I want you inside all his transactions: bank records, call logs, social media. If he so much as sneezes, I want to know about it."

"Yes, sir," Riya said without hesitation.

"Ayan, Vikram," Karan's gaze shifted to them. "You'll tail Stephen. Find out who he's meeting, what he's planning. Get me everything."

They both nodded.

"Mohit and I will hit the road," Karan went on. "We need to find out who's working the ground level, the ones making this operation possible from the inside."

He paused, then glanced back at Ayan.

"Good work. This is a solid lead."

Ayan gave a small nod. He knew: the real fight had just begun.

The team worked tirelessly, each chasing different leads, determined to untangle the web connecting Stephen Davis to the underground network.

Riya, buried in encrypted transactions and intercepted communications, kept stumbling upon the same alias; buried deep in financial trails, hidden within coded messages and offshore accounts. It wasn't a direct name, not at first. But the frequency of its appearance was impossible to ignore. Whoever this was, they weren't just another player in the game; they were steering it from the shadows.

Meanwhile, Karan and Mohit took to the streets, tracking movements in Andheri. Late one evening, amidst the usual rush of hawkers and pedestrians, their eyes locked onto a brief exchange.

A man in a loose hoodie, blending effortlessly into the crowd, brushed past another: this one dressed in an understated yet sharp manner, the kind of look that allowed him to move unnoticed without appearing out of place.

The interaction lasted no more than a second. A subtle flick of the wrist. A small, nondescript package slipped from one hand to another. No words. No unnecessary glances. But the tension in their postures was unmistakable.

Mohit's gaze hardened. "That guy in the hoodie," he murmured, barely moving his lips. "We've seen him before."

Karan followed his line of sight, recognition settling in. "Stephen's man."

At the same time, Ayan and Vikram had been tailing Stephen Davis himself. After hours of following his car through the city, they watched as it veered off its usual route, slipping into the dimly lit alleys of a neighborhood notorious for its underground dealings.

A sleek black SUV pulled up outside a rundown warehouse; no security detail, no corporate presence. Just a quiet meeting in a place where powerful figures weren't supposed to be seen.

Then Ayan spoke, his voice firm. "That car… I've seen it before." That moment stayed with him long after they had driven away.

Now, back in the operations room, the room was dimly lit, the glow of laptop screens casting faint light over scattered documents. The team had spent days combing through leads, piecing together fragments of information that, until now, had seemed disconnected.

Karan stood at the front, arms crossed, as Riya pulled up a series of files on the projector screen. "Everything we've uncovered," she began, "keeps circling back to a single entity. It wasn't obvious at first: different aliases, different transactions… but the patterns are there."

She tapped the screen, bringing up a web of connections. "These financial trails: offshore accounts, coded payments, high-value transactions… we kept running into the same shell companies."

Meanwhile, Captain Karan and Mohit had been following movements on the ground. "We tracked a deal happening in Andheri," Karan said, flipping through their reports. "One of Stephen's men picked up a package. Nothing major on the surface, but we confirmed it came from the same network that's been supplying high-end contraband."

Ayan had been silent throughout the briefing, his fingers tightening around a particular image among the scattered files: the picture of the black SUV from the warehouse.

Karan noticed. "Ayan, you okay?"

Ayan exhaled sharply, placing the photo down. "This car…" His tone was sharp, his body tense. "I've seen it before."

The others turned toward him.

"Anushka told me a black SUV had been following her days before the blast," he continued. "That same vehicle was at the explosion site. And even after that, it didn't disappear." His gaze locked onto Karan. "It was circling the Singhania mansion. I saw it at her funeral."

A heavy silence followed. The shift in Ayan's voice, the way his fingers curled against the table, made it clear to everyone. This wasn't just a case for him. It was personal.

Vikram leaned in. "Whoever owns that SUV wasn't just involved. They were watching everything. Before, during, and after."

Riya's fingers hovered over her keyboard. "I can run a trace…

She stopped as Karan spoke, his voice firm. "No need."

He met their gazes, his jaw tightening. Then, after a pause, he said the name that had been in front of them all along.

"That SUV belongs to Karim Mohammed."

The room went still.

Ayan's grip on the table tightened.

Mohit exhaled, rubbing a hand over his face. "The underworld king of Mumbai."

Vikram's expression darkened. "And the direct link to White Viper."

Karan nodded. "We've been chasing different trails, but they all lead back to him. The package in Andheri. His network. The offshore accounts."

Riya shifted uncomfortably. "If he's the one with the direct ties with the White Viper, this isn't going to be easy."

Ayan leaned forward slightly, his tone firm. "Then he's our way in. If we take him down, we cut off White Viper's closest link and force him into the open."

The days that followed were a blur of training, strategy, and relentless pursuit. There was no room for hesitation; if they were going after Karim Mohammed, they had to be ready.

The days leading up to the operation were relentless. Karim was heavily guarded, his movements calculated, his security airtight. There was no room for mistakes. Every second was spent refining their strategy, ensuring that when they struck, there would be no escape.

Riya kept a close watch on Stephen's activities, tracking his virtual presence: every financial transaction, encrypted message, and shift in his routine. He was the only loose thread connecting back to Karim, and any sudden change in his behavior could signal an opportunity.

Meanwhile, Ayan, Vikram, Karan, and Mohit focused entirely on the mission. Training was brutal: every scenario accounted for, every weakness eliminated. Karim's guards were professionals, and if it came down to a fight, they had to be better. Hours were spent drilling precision strikes, quick takedowns, and coordinated breaches. Every movement had to be instinctive.

Mohit handled the logistics, securing weapons, safehouses, and escape routes. If things went south, they needed a way out... fast. There was no room for hesitation.

As the final pieces fell into place, a quiet determination settled over them. The time for planning was almost over. Soon, they would make their move.

KARIM MOHAMMED
WHITE VIPER

TWENTY
THE SUCCESSOR

The air was thick with sweat, dust, and the metallic scent of blood. The torches along the perimeter flickered against the cold night, casting elongated shadows over the dirt ground. It was a place untouched by mercy, built on discipline and brutality.

Twelve men lay sprawled on the ground, bodies battered, groaning in pain. In the middle of them stood Kabir, his breath steady despite the exertion. Blood streaked his knuckles. The only sounds were the labored breaths of the fallen and the distant murmur of the camp beyond the training ground.

Then, slow claps cut through the silence.

Kabir didn't react immediately. He dragged a hand across his face, wiping away something that seemed like sweat, then paused briefly as his fingers came away stained with red. Without hesitation, he brushed it off and turned.

Ibrahim Al-Malik watched him, his expression calm, his one good eye gleaming with something between amusement and expectation. "You do know you're supposed to train them, not cripple them."

Kabir's gaze was steady. "Every punch that doesn't kill them makes them stronger." His voice was even, without pride or excuse. "We need warriors. Nothing less."

Ibrahim's attention flickered to the blood on Kabir's nose. "Twelve men in fifteen minutes... and you're bleeding." His tone was almost mocking. "Are you getting slower?"

Kabir wiped the blood away with his thumb, his movements precise, deliberate. "Must be the weather."

Ibrahim chuckled. "You sound like an old man." He gestured toward the unconscious men at Kabir's feet. "But I suppose they wouldn't agree."

Kabir said nothing, stepping over the fallen bodies, his stride measured, unhurried.

Ibrahim fell in step beside him, his tone shifting. "Amar remains in India. Useful for now." He studied Kabir as they walked. "But soon, the weight of this empire will shift. When it does, it needs someone strong enough to bear it."

Kabir kept walking without any response.

Ibrahim looked down at the fallen men, his tone laced with quiet disdain. "If you can stand, do it. If not, crawl to the water and wash the shame off your faces."

Kabir moved through the camp like a ghost: silent, but unmistakably felt by those around him. He had mastered the art of entering and exiting spaces without leaving a trace, slipping in and out like a shadow that never lingered. His every movement, every step, seemed to have a purpose that eluded the average observer. There were no wasted motions, no superfluous gestures... only precision.

His voice, when he spoke, carried both strength and wisdom, resonating with an authority that couldn't be ignored. Some respected him for it, recognizing the depth of experience behind every word. Others feared him, knowing that his silence spoke volumes, that his stillness was as dangerous as any action.

As Kabir passed by groups of men training, their eyes often lingered on him, but no one dared to approach. He was a figure of focus and discipline, a man who didn't need to assert his dominance with loud commands or public displays of power. His mere presence commanded respect, and when he did speak, it was with a calm, measured tone that held the weight of years... years of hardship, sacrifice, and a philosophy of survival.

When he entered the training area, the usual noise of fists and feet striking pads momentarily quieted. Kabir's gaze swept over the men, and they instinctively straightened. There was no announcement, no fanfare. He simply observed; his eyes calculating, his posture unwavering. The men continued their training, but with each glance from Kabir, they knew they were being measured. The silence around him spoke louder than any command could.

One of the younger trainees, eager to prove himself, threw a punch in Kabir's direction, hoping to catch him off guard. Kabir's response was immediate: an almost imperceptible shift of weight, a single fluid motion that sent the young man crashing to the ground, his pride bruised more than his body.

Kabir stood over him, unmoved. "Power without control is chaos," he said, his voice low, but carrying the weight of a truth that was understood by all who heard it. "Strength is not in force, but in the ability to guide it. If you can't control your own actions, how can you control anything else?"

He didn't wait for a response, nor did he need to. Kabir's words weren't for those who wanted to be led. They were for those who sought to understand, to grow stronger in both body and mind.

With a final glance at the men, Kabir turned and walked away, his presence fading into the distance, leaving behind a trail of silence. There was no applause, no acknowledgment from those around him, but the lesson had been delivered. Kabir didn't need recognition. His strength, wisdom, and authority were undeniable to those who understood the true meaning of power. And for those who didn't, his silence was a warning.

The next morning, the camp was still, the air heavy with the quiet hum of the morning. The first rays of light cast long shadows across the training grounds, painting everything in muted shades of gold. Kabir stood in the heart of the training ground, a remote part of the camp where nature and discipline merged. Towering trees surrounded him, their branches thick with leaves, and the air was thick with the scent of earth. His eyes scanned the setup: several rocks tied to the ends of ropes, swinging back and forth between the trees. The rocks were erratic, unpredictable, swaying at different speeds, some coming close, some retreating farther. This was no ordinary training. It was designed to test his reflexes, his speed, and his ability to read movement without thinking.

The sword in his hand gleamed in the morning light, the steel an extension of his will. Kabir stepped forward, moving between the fast-moving rocks with deliberate precision. His sword was an extension of his body, slicing through the air in perfect synchronization with his movements. Each swing was deliberate, with no hesitation and no wasted effort. His eyes locked onto the rocks, following their erratic paths, anticipating their next move, adapting to their rhythm in real-time.

His feet slid across the ground as he danced between the rocks, his body moving faster than thought itself. Kabir's mind was calm, focused. There was only the rhythm of the rocks and the sound of his breathing as he sliced through the air, the sword flashing like lightning. His movements were fluid, honed from years of training, his body operating on instinct, not conscious thought. His reflexes were sharp: faster than the rocks could swing, faster than any normal person could follow.

But then, suddenly, something changed.

Kabir's sword sliced through the air, but missed the target. One of the rocks grazed him. He froze for a brief moment, staring at it as if the mistake was something out of place.

"Hmm, interesting," he muttered, barely acknowledging the slip as he resumed his rhythm.

He continued, faster, more determined, but the rocks were coming too quickly now. His movements, once fluid and sharp, began to lag; just a fraction of a second, he lost his footwork.

The rocks, unpredictable as always, came crashing toward him. Kabir tried to dodge, but his foot slipped on the ground, and a rock struck him from behind. His sword flew out of his hand, landing some distance away.

He stood still for a moment, taking it all in, his breathing steady, then glanced at the fallen sword.

Then his eyes moved to the horizon, and without a hint of surprise, he said, "I see, so it's almost time."

Months passed. Every attempt to capture Karim had crumbled: political interference, unexpected roadblocks, or sheer force shielding him like an untouchable ghost. But Ayan had waited long enough. This time, there would be no escape.

The city was alive with its usual chaos, but for Ayan and his team, the world had shrunk to the dimly lit corridors of the abandoned industrial district. A storm was brewing... not in the skies but in the air thick with anticipation. Karim was close. Closer than he had ever been.

This was not just another attempt. This was the last attempt. If they failed, there wouldn't be another.

Karan adjusted his earpiece, voice calm but edged with steel. "Positions?"

"North exit secured," Vikram reported.

"South clear," Riya whispered.

Mohit's voice cut through. "Front entrance locked. No movement."

Ayan inhaled sharply. Karim had always been untouchable. Attempts to capture him had crumbled under political intervention, sudden roadblocks, or sheer force. His web of influence stretched far beyond the underworld: politicians, high-ranking officers, even international figures had protected him like a phantom no one could pin down.

But not tonight.

The team had worked for months, tracking his movements, bribing the right people, and cutting off his usual escape routes. Karim believed he was invincible, that another failed attempt was inevitable. But what he didn't know... what no one knew, was that Ayan had made sure this time, there would be no outside interference. No last-minute rescues. No political strings pulled.

Karim was in his safehouse, a heavily guarded fortress within a forgotten warehouse. He was surrounded by a dozen of his best men, each armed to the teeth. But Ayan's team wasn't walking into a trap. They had designed the battlefield themselves.

Karan gave the signal.

Ayan and Vikram moved first, planting explosives on the main power line. The moment the lights flickered, a single blast plunged the entire compound into darkness.

Then came the chaos.

Gunfire erupted. Karim's men scrambled, but their guns were useless against the tactical advantage Ayan's team had spent months preparing. The sound of suppressed gunfire cut through the confusion. Ayan moved in like a ghost, dispatching two guards before they even realized what hit them.

Inside, Karim's voice roared above the commotion. "Get me out of here! NOW!"

His guards rushed to escort him, but they had nowhere to go.

Riya's voice crackled in Ayan's earpiece. "Target heading to the underground exit."

Ayan was already moving. He reached the lower levels as Karim and his last remaining guard bolted for the hidden tunnel. Karim turned, sweat lining his forehead, a wildness in his eyes. He had escaped every time before. He had won every time before.

But this time, Ayan was waiting.

The fight was brutal. Karim's last man lunged, but Ayan sidestepped, taking him down in a swift, brutal strike. Karim tried to run, but Ayan caught him, slamming him against the cold metal wall.

"You're done," Ayan breathed.

Karim struggled, but he could see it: the inevitability, the end. The fear in his eyes was unmistakable.

For the first time, Karim had nowhere left to run.

This mission was so secretive that even high-ranking officials were unaware of its existence. To prevent political intervention like past failures, Ayan and his team decided to keep Karim hidden.

Captain Karan had a place: an abandoned military outpost far from prying eyes.

The room smelled of sweat and fear. Karim sat, wrists bound to the chair, his head hanging forward. His face was bruised, his lip split, and a fresh cut ran along his temple. The fluorescent light flickered above, casting harsh shadows across the damp concrete walls.

Karan paced before him, arms crossed. "You have one chance, Karim. Who is the White Viper?"

Karim let out a ragged breath, lifting his swollen eyes. Then, he smirked. "You think I'll just hand it over?"

Ayan's patience had worn thin. He stepped forward and grabbed Karim's jaw, forcing him to look up. "We're not asking. We're taking."

Karan signaled Vikram, who stepped behind Karim and pulled a plastic bag over his head. Within seconds, Karim thrashed against his restraints, his muffled screams filling the room. Ayan counted the seconds, watching his body convulse before Vikram finally ripped the bag off.

Karim gasped for air, coughing violently.

Karan leaned in, voice like ice. "Again. Who is the White Viper?"

Karim let out a dry chuckle, blood dripping from his mouth. "You... You think you're the first to try this?"

Ayan exhaled sharply, rolling up his sleeves. "No. But we'll be the last."

What followed was hours of psychological and physical torment. They switched between drowning him, beating him, and keeping him on the edge of consciousness; never letting him rest, never giving him a moment to collect his thoughts. They shattered his arrogance piece by piece.

And then, after days of resistance, Karim finally broke.

"The White Viper... his name is Amar."

Silence filled the room. But they weren't done.

"I met Amar over a year ago," Karim muttered, his voice hoarse. "Once a year, we have a gathering in a secret location near the border in Kashmir, where we meet Ibrahim."

Karan's eyes narrowed. "Who is 'we'?"

Karim hesitated before replying. "Me, Stephen Davis, and... and...

"Suresh Krishna," Ayan finished for him, his voice cold.

Karim exhaled sharply, avoiding Ayan's gaze. "Yes."

Karan pressed further. "Where do you meet?"

Karim licked his dry lips. "It's always a different location. We never know beforehand. We're blindfolded from the moment we enter Kashmir, but... It's always somewhere near the mountains."

Ayan, Vikram, Mohit, and Riya stood around Karim, listening intently.

Karan's voice was sharp. "What are your plans?"

"I don't know."

Ayan's fist connected with Karim's face, making him groan in pain. Blood dripped from his mouth.

"I really don't know!" Karim gasped. "I only do what they tell me! They pay me, give me weapons, and protect me from the law; that's all. Everything is planned by Suresh and Ibrahim."

Karan and Ayan exchanged a glance before Karan leaned in again. "Tell us about your last meeting."

Karim swallowed hard. "We were summoned because Suresh was furious about the recent failed missions. He wanted to change the strategy. Ibrahim... he wanted to make sure we didn't back out." Karim hesitated, his voice dropping lower. "That's when he introduced Amar: the one who planned the mall bombing months later. My job was to accommodate him and provide whatever he needed. That's all."

Karan's stare hardened. "Who else was there apart from you, Stephen, and Suresh?"

Karim exhaled sharply, his voice hoarse. "Ibrahim. And Kabir."

Karan's expression darkened. "Kabir Yusuf Ali? Why was he there?"

Karim barely lifted his head, his voice strained but certain. "He's Ibrahim's right hand. The one who's been running things long before Amar." He let out a slow, pained breath. "I heard he's next in line to lead. That's why Ibrahim sent Amar here, to execute this mission."

Ayan felt his breath hitch. They had always known Kabir was working for someone, but Ibrahim Al-Malik? The most feared name in the underworld? The weight of it settled in Ayan's chest like a stone.

Suddenly, Karim's phone vibrated on the table, the notification sound catching Vikram's attention. He picked it up, his eyes narrowing as he read the message. It was a location and a time, followed by two letters... WV.

"Sir, this just came in," Vikram said, showing the screen to Captain Karan.

Karan took one look at the message before turning to Karim. He held up the phone. "What is this?"

Karim hesitated.

Karan stood straight, then gave Ayan a small nod. No words were needed.

Ayan's fist shot forward, aiming for Karim's gut. But just before impact, Karim blurted out, "It's from him!"

Karim swallowed hard. "Amar," he said, his voice hoarse. "He wants to meet. This... this is how he communicates."

Ayan's heart pounded. "He's in Mumbai?"

Karim dragged in a breath, wincing. "Yes. He came back last week."

Silence hung heavy in the air.

"So another attack..." Mohit's voice was barely above a whisper.

Karan's grip tightened around the phone. His gaze bore into Karim. "Is that true?"

Karim nodded weakly. "Yes... But I don't know the details. I think... that's why he wants to meet."

For a moment, no one spoke. The weight of the revelation settled in. The room felt colder, the air thick with unspoken thoughts.

Karan exhaled sharply, pushing back the storm in his mind. Without a word, he motioned for the team to follow him into the other room. Once inside, he faced them, his jaw set, his eyes sharp with determination.

He took a deep breath.

"This is our chance," he said, his voice steady. "Tomorrow, we catch the White Viper."

The team reached the abandoned building on the outskirts of Andheri long before the scheduled time. Under the cover of darkness, they spread out, securing vantage points, setting traps, and placing surveillance. Every possible escape route was accounted for. Now, all that was left was to wait.

A black Scorpio rolled into the compound, its tires crunching against gravel. Amar stepped out first, scanning the empty surroundings, his sharp eyes narrowing. Four men followed, each armed. The silence felt unnatural.

Something was off.

Amar pulled out his phone and dialed Karim's number. No response. His gut twisted.

"Get in the car," he ordered, his voice tight. "We're leaving. Now."

The moment his men turned, a sharp crack echoed through the night.

A bullet from a sniper tore through one of them, his body dropping lifelessly to the ground.

Panic set in.

The remaining men scrambled for cover, pointing their guns wildly into the shadows, unsure where the shot had come from. Amar pressed himself against a pillar, his revolver drawn. His pulse pounded in his ears.

Another shot rang out.

The man hiding behind the Scorpio slumped over, blood pooling beneath him. Only three left.

Amar cursed under his breath and reached for his phone again. No signal. The network was jammed.

"Damn it!" he hissed, frustration boiling over.

He turned to his men. "Run to the exit! Now!"

The moment they moved, an explosion erupted at the entrance. The shockwave sent debris flying, sealing off their only way out.

Dust and smoke clouded the air.

Trapped.

A slow grin spread across Amar's face. His adrenaline spiked. Instead of fear, excitement coursed through him.

A laugh rumbled from his chest.

"Are you so afraid of me that you have to hide in the shadows?" His voice echoed through the ruins. "Fight like men, you cowards!"

Gun in hand, he stepped into the open. His men followed, weapons raised.

Two gunshots cut through the night.

Both men behind him collapsed, bullets clean through their skulls.

Silence.

Amar exhaled sharply, his fingers tightening around his revolver.

Then, from the shadows, two figures emerged.

Karan. Ayan.

Without hesitation, Amar aimed at Karan.

Before he could pull the trigger, a shot rang out from his left.

Pain exploded through his wrist as the gun was ripped from his grasp, clattering to the floor. He clutched his bleeding hand, teeth clenched.

Karan stared him down. "We're not cowards," he said coldly. "And we're not stupid enough to prove it."

Amar growled, his left hand reaching behind for the knife strapped to his back.

"Before you move," Karan warned, his voice calm, "know that there's a sniper locked on your head. Two more guns aimed at you from your left and right."

He tilted his head slightly.

"So if I were you... I wouldn't move."

Just like that, a squad that had only recently stepped into the field had managed to capture one of the most feared terrorists. They brought Amar back to the same place where they had been holding Karim.

He was unconscious when they carried him in; sedating him had clearly taken some effort. They tied him to a chair in a different room, securing the restraints tightly. Then, they waited.

Hours passed. The room remained eerily silent, save for the occasional creak of a chair or the faint sound of someone shifting their weight.

Then, finally, Amar stirred. A sharp inhale, a twitch of his fingers, then his head lifted slowly. His eyes flickered open, adjusting to the dim lighting. And the first thing he saw... Ayan.

A smirk tugged at Amar's lips as recognition dawned. "You must be Ayan Yusuf Ali," he said, his tone almost amused. "Big brother talks a lot about you."

A hard fist met his face before he could say another word. His head snapped to the side, blood trickling from his lip.

Ayan's voice was low, controlled. "Be careful with your words."

From behind, Karan stepped forward, his presence heavy in the tense room. "Now that you're awake," he said, voice steady, "let's talk."

Amar exhaled sharply, shifting against his restraints. Then, despite the situation, despite the pain, his smirk returned. He ran his tongue over his wounded lip, tasting the blood.

"Sure," he said slowly, tilting his head. "What's for dinner?"

Karan smirked. "Let's see if you make it till then."

For the first time, Amar's expression faltered. His smirk didn't vanish completely, but something in his eyes flickered: annoyance, maybe. Or realization.

He leaned back slightly. "You think you can keep me here?" His voice was steady, but there was an underlying edge to it now. "I'll be out in minutes. You better keep your phones charged."

Karan chuckled, shaking his head. "Oh, you think this is a government facility where your sugar daddies will come running to bail you out?"

He crouched slightly, bringing himself to Amar's level. His next words were slow, deliberate.

"Buddy, we're off the grid. No one's coming. No one's gonna hear you scream."

A brief silence followed.

Amar's eyes darted around the room, taking in his surroundings with more focus this time. The lack of official infrastructure, the absence of outside interference. It was only now sinking in.

Still, he masked it well. Letting out a short chuckle, he feigned nonchalance. "Oh, so we're playing off the books now?" He lifted a brow, looking directly at Ayan. "Going bad cop, huh?" A slow grin spread across his face. "Just like your big brother."

Ayan stepped forward, his fists clenching.

Before he could strike, Riya walked in from the other room. "Sir," she said to Karan, "I went through his phone. There's nothing useful. It's a brand-new device, only had Karim's number. He must have another phone or a different way of contacting his people."

Karan sighed. "I see. Alright. I need to brief the higher-ups, cover our tracks." He glanced at the team. "Riya, you stay here. Mohit too. I'm taking Vikram with me."

Then, he looked at Ayan. "Just don't kill him before I get back, alright?"

Ayan didn't look away from Amar. His jaw tightened.

"Yes, sir."

Ayan, Riya, and Mohit sat in the next room, going through the documents and items recovered from Karim's place and Amar's belongings. The dim light cast long shadows over the scattered papers, some marked with foreign scripts, others with numbers and coded messages.

Riya stood near Ayan, flipping through a file. She hesitated, glancing at him from the corner of her eye. The silence in the room made her pause even longer, but eventually, she spoke.

"Ayan..." Her voice was careful. "Can I ask you something? If you don't mind?"

Ayan, still focused on the papers in front of him, barely looked up. "Yes? Go ahead."

Riya pursed her lips, choosing her words. "What's your connection to all this?" she finally asked. "I mean, we've kind of understood this is personal... but no one really wanted to ask. Now, though, we're deep into this, and understanding the full picture might help the team."

Mohit looked up from his side, sensing the weight behind her words.

The room fell silent again.

Ayan didn't respond immediately. His fingers rested on the edge of a paper, his eyes fixed on a list of names, but his mind had drifted far from the document.

For a moment, it seemed like he wouldn't answer.

Then, without looking up, he said, "Kabir Yusuf Ali."

The way he said that name, low and measured, yet carrying something heavy, made both Riya and Mohit straighten slightly.

Ayan exhaled through his nose, finally lifting his gaze. "He's my brother."

The room went silent for a moment. He continued, "Well... I wouldn't really call him that," he said, his voice calm but laced with something unreadable. "But technically, he is."

Riya and Mohit exchanged a glance, the weight of his words settling in. The room, already quiet, felt even heavier.

Riya took a moment to process what Ayan had just said. She had suspected this was personal, but hearing it out loud was something else entirely. She opened her mouth, searching for the right words, but before she could speak, Mohit jumped in.

"Then who is Anushka?" he asked.

Ayan's gaze flickered to Riya, then to Mohit. His expression didn't change.

"She was a classmate," he said simply. "A good person."

Riya hesitated before speaking. "So that blast in the mall... the one that killed her, that's why you've been so determined to capture him."

Ayan exhaled. "Kind of."

Mohit frowned. "Kind of?"

Ayan's voice was steady, but there was something distant in his tone. "The blast was meant for her. But she wasn't the only one I lost that day."

Riya's brow furrowed. "Then who?"

Ayan looked away, his jaw tightening. "Doesn't matter."

Silence settled between them. They didn't need to push further; they understood. This wasn't just about Anushka. There was something, someone, that had left a much deeper scar.

Mohit shook his head. "I don't get it. After everything you just said... how can you be this calm around Amar?"

Ayan's eyes darkened. "It's not that I don't hate him," he said. "But he's just a pawn. A puppet being used by people far more dangerous." His voice was cold, resolute.

"I want to cut off the head, not the tail."

The next moment, his phone started vibrating in his hand. The ringing cut through the stillness of the moment, pulling his attention away from the silence around him. He glanced at the screen... an unknown number.

He picked up.

The voice on the other end, "Is this Ayan Ali?"

"Yes, Who is this?"

"This is from Apollo Hospital. Are you related to Mr. Raghav Murthi?"

Ayan's chest tightened. Panic crept into his voice. "Yes. What happened?"

"Sir, Mr. Murthi has been admitted here. It's serious. Could you please come?"

The words hung in the air for a moment, thick with tension. Ayan swallowed hard, trying to steady his breathing. "I'll be there right away."

He turned to Riya and Mohit. "I need to go. Raghav is in trouble."

They understood the urgency from the look on his face.

They both nodded, understanding the gravity of the situation without needing any more explanation. Mohit's voice was steady as he reassured Ayan, "Don't worry. We'll handle things here."

Riya added quietly, "I'll inform Karan sir."

With a curt nod, Ayan wasted no time. He rushed out of the room, the heavy weight of dread in his chest pulling him forward.

Ayan stepped into the hospital and immediately spotted Mr. Sharma, a retired teacher and Raghav's neighbor for over twenty-five years. Their eyes met, and Ayan hurried toward him.

"What happened?" he asked, breathless.

Mr. Sharma's face was pale. "I heard gunshots. When I went to check, I saw a car speeding away from your house. I called an ambulance and brought Raghav and the guard here."

"Where is he now?" Ayan asked urgently.

"He's in the operating theatre," Mr. Sharma said, his voice shaking.

Ayan nodded. "Thank you. Please don't panic; I'll talk to the doctors."

He turned towards the operation theatre and waited.

Minutes stretched into an eternity. Then, a doctor stepped out.

"There was a bullet near his heart. We managed to remove it, and he's out of danger for now. But we can't say anything for certain yet."

Ayan sat in the waiting area of the hospital, his elbows resting on his knees, hands clasped together. The smell of antiseptic filled the air, mixing with the distant beeping of machines. His mind was clouded with memories: Raghav standing strong, guiding him, never showing weakness. And now, he lay in a hospital bed, fighting for his life.

Mr. Sharma sat beside him, his face filled with worry. "He's a strong man, Ayan," he said quietly. "He will fight through this."

Ayan gave a small nod but said nothing.

Hours passed. The weight of exhaustion pressed on him, but his mind wouldn't let him rest.

Then, his phone rang.

Ayan straightened and pulled out his phone. Captain Karan.

He answered immediately. "Sir?"

Karan's voice was tense. "Ayan, I know it's a bad time. I heard about Raghav sir. But we have a situation, and we need you here."

Ayan's grip tightened. "What happened?"

Karan exhaled sharply. "There's been an explosion. I'll brief you once you're here."

Ayan stood up instantly, his chest tightening. He glanced at the ICU doors, where Raghav lay unconscious. First this, and now an explosion? His instincts screamed that this wasn't a coincidence.

He turned to Mr. Sharma. "Please stay here. If anything changes, call me."

Mr. Sharma nodded. "Go, Ayan. Do what you need to do."

Ayan took one last look toward Raghav's room before rushing out of the hospital.

Smoke was still rising from what had once been the safehouse. Now, it was nothing but charred debris, crumbling walls, and the distant wail of sirens. The fire had been put out, but the stench of burning metal and flesh lingered in the air.

Ayan stepped out of the car, eyes locked on the wreckage. For a moment, he just stared.

Vikram stood a few feet away, looking lost; his hands shaking, his face pale.

Then, Karan approached. His expression was unreadable, but there was something heavy in his eyes. Guilt. Loss. Failure.

Ayan's voice was low, controlled. "What happened?"
Karan didn't hesitate. "...We lost."

Karan nodded, jaw tight. "Whoever did this... they didn't just want to kill Amar and Karim. They wanted to erase them. No remains. No trace."

Ayan stared at the ruins, the sinking weight of reality pressing against his chest. Someone had silenced Amar before he could talk.

"What about Mohit and Riya?" Ayan asked quietly.

Karan didn't answer right away. He just gave a slow nod, his expression tight, eyes clouded with emotion.

Ayan's fists clenched tightly. The one lead he had to end it all... gone. His only chance at reaching Kabir, lost. And on top of that, two teammates, too.

He stood frozen, his gaze fixed on the wreckage, the weight of everything he had lost pressing down on him. Lost. Again.

TWENTY-ONE
A NEW BEGINNING

A few weeks had passed since that harrowing night. Raghav was slowly recovering, his strength returning bit by bit, but the road to full recovery was still a long one. The hospital room, with its sterile smell and the faint hum of machines, had become a familiar space to Ayan. He had stayed by Raghav's side since the incident, coming in daily to check on him, offering whatever support he could. The rest of the day, however, was dedicated to his missions, his mind consumed by the work that had to be done, even as his heart remained tethered to the hospital room.

Raghav's eyes were now open, and though he was weak, he had begun to speak again, his voice hoarse but steady. Ayan sat beside him, his thoughts running in circles as he stared at the man who had been his guide, his protector, and now, the only remaining tether to a past that felt increasingly distant.

The silence in the room felt heavy, a weight neither of them knew how to lift. But then, Ayan broke it, his voice quiet yet filled with urgency. "Raghav," he said, eyes searching the older man's face. "What happened that night? What really happened?"

Raghav turned his head slowly, his eyes distant as if recalling the nightmare was painful. He took a breath, wincing slightly, but continued. "I'm not sure who they were... I was in my study room when I heard the gunshot. Instincts kicked in, and I grabbed my gun. I went downstairs to check it out, but when I opened the door, they stormed in. There were four of them. I shot one, but the others were quick. One of them had a gun too... and he shot me. They were wearing masks, so I couldn't see their faces." He paused, as if replaying the moment in his mind.

Ayan felt his heart race, his fists tightening around the edges of his chair. "What were they looking for, Raghav?" he asked, his voice barely a whisper.

Raghav's breath was shallow, his eyes fluttering as he tried to recall more. "I think they were after my old case files. They wanted to know where I used to get the intel for the attacks... the ones our team used to stop. I think they were trying to find out who I was working with."

Ayan's brow furrowed in confusion. "Were the details of those intel in those documents?"

Raghav shook his head slowly, his gaze vacant. "No. I never wrote them down. I kept everything in my head, just in case something like this happened. I knew the risks."

Ayan's mind raced, the pieces not quite fitting together. "Then where did that intel come from, Raghav?"

Raghav hesitated, his hand trembling slightly as he moved to adjust himself on the bed. "I've been in this game for a long time, Ayan. I have my resources... people who work quietly, behind the scenes. That's where the intel came from."

Ayan's frustration grew. "We're in the middle of nowhere right now, Raghav. We could really use those resources, those connections."

Raghav's expression softened with regret. "I don't think my resources will be of any help to you now, Ayan. I've lost communication with them a while ago. I'm not sure what's going on anymore."

The words hit Ayan like a cold slap, and for a moment, he simply stared at Raghav, disappointment settling deep in his chest. He had come hoping for answers, for some sort of plan, but instead, he was met with uncertainty. The man he trusted, the man who had always been the source of his strength, seemed powerless.

Ayan stood up from the chair, his shoulders heavy with the weight of it all. Without saying another word, he left the hospital room, the echo of Raghav's helplessness following him out the door.

Ayan left the hospital with a heavy heart. The cool evening air hit him as he stepped outside, the weight of Raghav's condition still pressing on him. He had hoped for more clarity, but Raghav's words only left him with more questions and less hope. There was no solid lead. No answers. Just uncertainty.

The failed mission continued to haunt Ayan, casting a shadow over everything. The operation that had resulted in the deaths of two of his team members had led to Captain Karan's suspension, with a full investigation now underway. Both Ayan and Vikram were cleared of direct blame, having merely followed orders from their superiors. But that didn't change the fact that they were now sidelined, left in limbo.

Ayan had been reassigned to a new squad: a regular army team, with no ties to anti-terrorism. The missions were mundane: securing perimeters, routine patrols, and logistical tasks. Nothing like the high-risk, high-reward work he had been trained for. He had been accustomed to chasing down leads, breaking through walls of danger, and fighting terrorism on the front lines. Now, it felt like everything had come to a screeching halt.

Vikram had been reassigned to a new squad as well, leaving Ayan alone in this new world, one that felt foreign to him. The regular army didn't offer the thrill, the urgency, or the purpose he craved. He had made it clear to his superiors that he wanted to return to the Anti-Terrorist squad to continue the fight against terrorism, but with the investigation still ongoing, that was impossible.

Ayan's frustration grew every day as he woke up, went through the motions of his routine, and returned to the same empty feeling by nightfall. He wasn't part of the fight anymore, wasn't chasing down Kabir or investigating the leads that had once burned in his veins. Instead, he was just... there.

Every day, he tried to push his frustration aside, focusing on the menial tasks in front of him, but it was hard to ignore the gnawing sense that he was wasting his time, that he was stuck. Stuck in a world that had no place for him, stuck in a place where his skills, his purpose, meant nothing. The clock was ticking, but Ayan couldn't escape this standstill, and every moment felt like another lost opportunity.

A few weeks had passed since that night. Since everything changed. The morning was colder than usual. Ayan noticed it the moment he stepped outside, the crisp air brushing against his skin as he zipped up his jacket. Almost two years. It didn't feel real. Time had passed, but the weight of it remained the same, sitting heavily on his chest, unshaken.

He hadn't planned on going there. Not yet. The thought had been in his mind for weeks, but he had pushed it aside every time. Would it even make a difference? Would it change anything?

But when he woke up that morning, he found himself reaching for his keys, his mind made up before he could even question it.

Now, as he stood outside the orphanage gates, he hesitated.

It looked the same. The same faded blue paint on the walls, the same rusted hinges on the gate that creaked whenever it moved. He could hear faint laughter from inside, children playing just as they always did. For them, life had moved forward. It always did.

He let out a slow breath and pushed the gate open.

The moment he stepped inside, memories surfaced. Siva's voice, his laughter, the way he used to call out to the kids like they were his own little siblings. Ayan had never understood how he did it: how he had so much to give despite having so little himself.

He had only been here a handful of times. Once, on Siva's birthday, and a few other weekends when Siva had insisted. "Come on, Ayan! You'll like it. These kids need a role model, and let's be honest, you look scary enough to make them listen." Ayan had called him an idiot then, but he had gone anyway, standing at the edge of the playground while Siva played cricket with the kids, his energy never fading.

That was the thing about Siva. He had a way of pulling people in, even when they didn't want to be pulled.

Ayan hadn't expected to see anyone else here today. But as he stepped into the main hall, he saw them.

Imtiaz. Arun. Meenakshi.

They turned when they heard him enter. For a moment, there was silence.

Meenakshi was the first to speak. "You came."

Ayan only nodded. He didn't know what to say.

It wasn't awkward, though. They understood. They always had.

A small cake sat on the wooden table, its candles unlit. It was simple: chocolate, with a few decorations on top. Siva would have complained. "Just one cake? Where's the backup?" He would have said it with that mischievous grin of his, pretending to be serious before breaking into laughter.

One of the older boys stepped forward and lit the candles. The room grew quiet as the small flames flickered, casting a warm glow.

A little girl, no older than six, stepped closer to the table, her tiny fingers clutching the edge as she tilted her head to read the words written on the cake.

"Happy birthday, Siva bhaiya," she murmured softly.

The name lingered in the air for a moment, fragile yet heavy.

Then, one by one, the kids started to hum the familiar tune, their voices quiet at first, hesitant, before growing stronger.

Ayan stood at the back, watching.

The rest of the day passed in a blur of quiet moments. They played the games Siva used to love: football in the courtyard, board games inside. Ayan wasn't good at any of it, but the kids didn't care. They laughed, pulling him into their world, the way Siva once did.

At some point, he found himself in the kitchen, standing beside Meenakshi as she stirred a pot of rice. He didn't know how, but he ended up chopping vegetables while the cook gave instructions. It felt strange. Domestic. Like a life that didn't belong to him.

But it felt right, too.

Even in his absence, Siva was here.

As the evening approached, Ayan stepped outside, needing air. The sky had started to darken, the last light of the day fading into shades of orange and purple. The orphanage felt quieter now, the sounds of laughter dimming as the kids grew tired.

Then, from a distance, he saw it.

A small memorial stood at the far end of the courtyard. Siva's name was engraved on a simple plaque, surrounded by flowers. It wasn't a real grave; there was never a body to be buried, but the orphanage had made this place for the children to visit, to feel like he was still close.

Ayan watched as Imtiaz, Arun, and Meenakshi stood near it, placing flowers on the plaque. The kids followed, some whispering small prayers, others just standing there in silence.

Ayan stayed back.

He had made a promise to himself. He would only visit Siva when it was over: when the ones responsible were gone, when he had finished what he started.

Until then, he wouldn't stand before him.

So he turned and walked away.

Despite the weight of his responsibilities in the army, Ayan made it a point to visit Raghav as often as he could. Some days, it was early mornings before duty. Other days it was late nights, after long shifts. On weekends or days off, he stayed longer, sometimes past midnight, even sleeping on the stiff bench just outside the room.

It became routine. Not out of obligation, but out of something deeper.

Raghav had grown weaker over the past few weeks. His body was no longer the strong frame that once carried the weight of a city's safety. Some days, he would look through the window with a soft blanket wrapped around him, staring out as if counting seconds. Other days, he barely had the strength to talk, his words trailing off into silence.

Ayan noticed something else too, something in Raghav's eyes. A quiet struggle, like he was fighting an internal battle. It wasn't just illness. It was hesitation. Guilt. A desire to speak, but something was holding him back.

One evening, while Ayan sat beside him flipping through an old newspaper, Raghav turned to him and asked, "Why are you always here?"

Ayan looked up, caught off guard by the sudden question.

"There are people who can take care of me," Raghav said. "You should concentrate on your duty. You don't owe me this much."

Ayan didn't respond at first. His eyes lowered to the floor, lips tightening slightly. Then, he let out a long breath and spoke quietly at first, but clearly.

"I do," he said. "You just don't know how much."

Raghav tilted his head slightly, confused.

"I've spent most of my life running from the past. Hiding it. Burying it. Acting like it didn't touch me." Ayan's voice was steady, but there was something raw beneath it. "You saw all of that. And still, you didn't walk away."

He paused.

"When I lost everything, I didn't just lose a family; I lost a reason to live. Then you found me. Took me in. Gave me something I hadn't had in a long time... a home. A name. A purpose."

Raghav blinked, his eyes glistening now.

"You're not just a guardian to me, Raghav. You're like a father to me."

Raghav turned his face slightly, quickly wiping his eyes as though adjusting his position.

"I don't say these things. I never have," Ayan admitted. "But you should know... You should know that you matter to me. That you're the reason I'm still standing."

For a few seconds, Raghav looked at him... truly looked, and what he saw in Ayan's eyes was something he'd never seen before: vulnerability. Love. Fear.

"I'm here for you now," Ayan added. "My focus is to help you get back on your feet. After that... I'll return to my work. I'm close, Raghav... very close."

For a few seconds, Raghav looked at him, truly looked, as though he were caught in a storm of memories and fears. Then his gaze began to drift. His hand trembled.

"Ayan…" he whispered.

But before he could say more, his body tensed. His breathing became uneven. He clutched at his chest, eyes wide and full of panic.

"Raghav!" Ayan shot up and called out, "Doctor! Nurse!"

A nurse rushed in, followed closely by a doctor. After a quick examination, the doctor said urgently, "He's having a stroke. We need to take him to the ICU now."

Raghav was immediately moved to a stretcher. Ayan walked beside him as the nurse pushed the stretcher through the hospital corridors. He held Raghav's hand, trying to mask the fear in his eyes, but it was there. Raw. Real. Fear of losing someone again.

Raghav was trying to speak. His mouth moved, his throat working, but no sound came. And then, just before they reached the ICU doors, he managed to get out a few words.

"You must know the truth," he rasped. "I… I can't die without you knowing it…"

Before he could finish, the nurse stepped between them. "Sir, please wait here."

The grip on Ayan's hand loosened.

The ICU doors swung open.

And Raghav disappeared behind them.

Ayan stood there, frozen in place. The metallic thud of the door closing felt like it echoed through his chest. He stared at it, unmoving, the unfinished sentence circling in his mind like a storm.

You must know the truth…

His thoughts were racing, but his body felt numb. What was Raghav trying to say? What truth?

The questions piled on top of each other as Ayan sank into the nearest chair, his eyes never leaving the closed door in front of him.

Two days passed.

Raghav's condition slowly stabilized, and the crisis faded into a haze of quiet monitoring and guarded optimism. The doctors reassured Ayan that the worst had passed, though Raghav would still need close observation.

Ayan hadn't left the hospital since the stroke. He hadn't eaten properly, hadn't changed clothes. His uniform was wrinkled and stained, his eyes rimmed with sleeplessness. He kept vigil outside the ICU, only speaking when necessary, watching the door like it might open with a new answer at any moment.

Eventually, one of the nurses who had seen him every day approached gently. "You should go home," she said. "Just for a little while. Rest. Bring back some things for him. He'll need fresh clothes, maybe something familiar."

Ayan didn't answer immediately. He sat still, the nurse waiting patiently beside him. Finally, he nodded, standing with slow, heavy movements.

Reluctantly, he left the hospital, the sound of his boots echoing down the hallway as he made his way to Raghav's home, carrying nothing but fatigue, confusion, and the last words that refused to leave his mind.

The sun was already dipping low by the time Ayan reached Raghav's house.

The hallway was in disarray. A flower vase had been knocked over. Shoe racks and drawers were left ajar. Papers were scattered across the floor like fallen leaves. The silence wasn't peaceful...it was unsettling.

He moved deeper inside.

When he reached the study, his heart sank.

The room was a mess. The usually pristine bookshelves were disrupted, and several books, thrown carelessly to the floor. Drawers had been yanked open, files tossed aside. It was clear the men who came for Raghav had ransacked this place too.

Still, he stepped inside, navigating through the chaos. He bent down, picking up the crossword book Raghav always kept nearby. It was torn at the corner but intact. Then he spotted the reading glasses beneath the overturned recliner. He gathered a few clean clothes, some of Raghav's favorite woolen socks, and the shawl he liked to keep draped over his legs. Then he went to the kitchen, pulled out a few containers of soup and porridge he had prepared weeks ago, checked the expiry dates, and packed them neatly.

The silence around him was almost too much. For a moment, he just stood there in the hallway, gripping the edge of the dining table, eyes shut.

He should've felt relief. Raghav was alive. Out of danger, at least for now. But that sentence, the one Raghav couldn't finish, hung heavy in the air, like a storm cloud refusing to break.

Suddenly, his phone rang.

The sharp vibration cut through the silence like a knife. Ayan blinked, disoriented, and looked at the screen. Captain Karan.

His stomach tightened.

He answered immediately. "Sir?"

Karan's voice was low, urgent. "Ayan... just got a word from someone in the old squad. We've got a lead."

Ayan stood up, fully awake now. "On who?"

"Ibrahim. And Kabir. They're moving in tonight. That's all I can tell you right now. The rest is classified, even for me."

Ayan's pulse quickened. His breath hitched. "You're serious?"

"I think this is it," Karan said. Then, after a pause, "Stay alert. I'll try to update you if I hear anything."

The call ended.

Ayan stood frozen, his phone still pressed to his ear long after the call had disconnected.

He felt like something inside him had been set on fire. A flicker of hope, burning hot against the layers of exhaustion and frustration he had carried for so long.

They were finally making a move.

And he wasn't part of it.

The helplessness hit him like a punch. He paced the living room, fists clenched. He tried calling Karan again... but no response. Then someone else from his unit. Then another. No one picked up. They were already in the field. Out of reach.

He turned on the news. Nothing. Switched to another channel. Still nothing.

The silence was unbearable.

The entire night, he didn't sleep. He kept switching channels, refreshing news apps, and messaging his contacts. Every time the phone buzzed, his heart would leap, hoping for an update. But there was nothing.

The waiting became a torment of its own.

By midnight, fatigue began to creep in. He hadn't slept in days, hadn't eaten properly. His body gave up before his mind did. At some point around 3 a.m., with the news still murmuring in the background and his phone clutched in his hand, Ayan finally slipped into a restless sleep on the couch.

He jolted awake around 7, the phone buzzing relentlessly in his hand.

His eyes fluttered open, blurry, disoriented. The phone lit up with Captain Karan's name, but by the time his thumb swiped across the screen, it had already gone to missed call.

He stared at it, heart pounding.

Then his eyes dropped lower.

He opened the notification bar. Dozens of messages.

"Check the news."

"Turn on the TV, now."

Heart thudding, Ayan grabbed the remote and flipped on the television.

There it was.

Breaking News: Ibrahim Al-Malik Confirmed Dead.

The words hit him like a wave. He stared, frozen, as the screen filled with footage: blurry night shots, helicopters, armored trucks.

The reporter's voice carried through the room:

"Last night, in a high-risk operation, the Indian Army surrounded Ibrahim Al-Malik's base in a remote mountainous region in Kashmir. A total of 36 armed terrorists were killed in the crossfire, including the terrorist leader himself. No casualties were reported from the Indian side."

Ayan leaned forward, gripping the edge of the table.

Another headline rolled in, colder, sharper:

"Evidence Links Ibrahim to Political and Business Elites."

The camera cut to a press conference. Authorities confirmed the raid had yielded hard evidence of Ibrahim's ties to Suresh Krishna, leader of the opposition party, Mumbai tycoon Stephen Devassy, and underground mafia boss Karim Mohammed. Arrest warrants had already been issued.

"Names of several businessmen and politicians are being verified and will be disclosed shortly," the anchor said. "Many have already been taken into custody."

And then came the part Ayan dreaded most:

"The Hunt for Kabir Yusuf Ali Continues."

The anchor's tone shifted... tense, cautious.

"According to military reports, Kabir Yusuf Ali was not present at the time of the raid. Authorities believe he may have fled prior to the operation or was stationed at a different base. However, in the raid, the army retrieved extensive files: detailing the full scope of Ibrahim's organisation, its safehouses, international contacts, and active sleeper cells."

Ayan didn't blink. He barely breathed.

"The data has been handed over to intelligence agencies across borders. Local police have already begun coordinated arrests of sleeper agents across multiple states."

Another pause.

"Today marks a historic victory for India."

The anchor smiled, a rehearsed gesture. "Well done, Indian Army."

But Ayan wasn't smiling.

He sat in silence. The news kept playing, but he had already stopped hearing it.

His thoughts were elsewhere.

Kabir wasn't there.

Somehow, even after all this, the ghost of his brother had managed to slip through the cracks again.

Ayan returned to the hospital, the noise of the world still ringing in his ears. He carried a small bag with Raghav's clothes, his reading glasses, and the crossword book that still had a half-finished puzzle from a few weeks back.

He handed it over to the nurse without a word.

His face was veiled, but the weight of what he'd seen, what he'd heard, pressed down on his shoulders.

Afterward, he went straight to see Captain Karan.

The front gate was slightly open, lights dimmed inside. Ayan found him on the veranda, seated with a cup of tea, eyes fixed on nothing in particular.

"I don't know much," Karan said, voice low. "The mission was led by Major Balveer Singh. Got a lead, acted on it fast. That's all I've heard."

Ayan's brows lifted slightly.

"I know him," he muttered. "He used to come to see Raghav when I was young. I also spoke to him at Raghav's retirement party."

Ayan didn't linger. He left shortly after.

He visited the army camp, hoping for answers. There were more vehicles than usual, and the place was buzzing with movement.

He spotted someone familiar near the training grounds... Vikram.

It had been a while since Ayan had seen him. They exchanged a nod. Ayan approached.

"Is Balveer here?" Ayan asked.

Vikram paused, looked at him, and nodded slowly... understanding exactly why he was asking.

"He's in Delhi. Debriefing the PM," he said. "You won't find him here."

"You know anything?"

"Only what's in the news. I wasn't part of it. I just train the rookies now."

Another dead end.

By evening, Ayan was back at the hospital. The sun dipped behind the buildings. Inside, everything was quiet. Still.

He sat next to Raghav's bed again, the steady beep of the monitor his only company. His voice was barely audible.

"What are you hiding, Raghav?"

TWENTY-TWO
THE SHOWDOWN

The next day began like the last. The same weight in his chest. The same heavy footsteps toward the camp.

Ayan checked again; no word on Balveer.

Hope flickered. Then faded.

Again.

And again.

Until, finally, at 3:06 p.m., the hospital called.

"Commissioner Raghav has started speaking. He wishes to speak with you."

The sentence struck like a lightning bolt, tearing through the thick fog of uncertainty. Ayan shot up from his seat, the air suddenly lighter, his limbs trembling with urgency.

He turned to leave.

His phone rang again.

Unknown number.

He stared at it, heart pulsing like a war drum.

He answered.

Silence.

And then ...

"Hello, Brother."

Ayan froze.

The voice. That voice. Unmistakable.

Low, calm, detached... but intimate. It crawled out from the cracks in his memory like a ghost.

"Kabir..."

"I hear you are still chasing ghosts," the voice replied, tinged with amusement.

Ayan stepped out of the makeshift tent, the busy murmur of the camp fading behind him as if someone had turned the volume down on the world. Sunlight gave way to a looming shadow.

"Where are you?" he asked. The rage in his voice had no weight. Only disbelief.

Kabir chuckled. It wasn't a laugh. It was a breath. A memory.

"Let's end it where it all began," he said, every word deliberate. "Come home, brother."

Click.

The line went dead.

Ayan stood motionless, phone still pressed to his ear, letting everything sink in.

Night descended like a silent predator as Ayan approached the house.

The family mansion stood at the edge of the street like a forgotten monument. Its windows were lifeless eyes. The gates groaned open as he stepped through, their hinges crying out in protest, as if the house itself resented his return.

Vines curled around the once-glorious pillars. The lawn was overgrown. The air hung heavy, scented with wet dust and memory.

The front door had been left ajar; a deliberate gesture. It waited.

Ayan stepped through.

Inside, the past assaulted him.

The walls were peeling but familiar. The chandelier still hung, its crystals dull and cobwebbed. The smell: a strange blend of old incense, rotting wood, and something metallic, clung to the air like death.

He passed the living room. Nothing had moved. The broken frame on the floor, the blood-stained rug, the shattered vase: all preserved in decay.

The stairwell loomed ahead.

And there, standing at the window, silhouetted against the moonlight, was Kabir

He had his back turned, as if posing. As if waiting to be noticed.

"You came," Kabir said softly.

Ayan didn't respond. He walked in, each step louder than the last.

Kabir turned. His face emerged from the shadows.

He looked... older. Pale. Thinner. His beard had grown, streaked with gray. But those eyes... those cruel, clever eyes, had not changed.

They stared at each other.

Two brothers.

Two worlds apart.

"You finally found me, Congratulations," Kabir said, tilting his head slightly.

Ayan's voice was a blade.

"How can you stand here after doing what you did?"

"Because I did what was necessary."

The calmness, the serenity in his voice... it infuriated Ayan.

"Necessary? You butchered them. Our family. Our people. And now you're here like nothing happened."

Kabir's eyes didn't waver. "I see no glory in what I did. But I see purpose."

Ayan clenched his jaw. "So you came here to kill me too?"

"Yes," Kabir said without hesitation. "You are the last tie. The last illusion of the life I left behind."

Ayan's breath hitched. "And you're not even sorry."

Kabir tilted his head slightly, with a calm expression. "Regret is for those who lose sight of the goal. I never did."

It boiled over.

Ayan charged.

Kabir didn't move. Not at first.

Ayan swung his fist with all his might, but Kabir ducked effortlessly, moving like a shadow in the dimly lit room. He countered instantly, a sharp, precise strike to Ayan's ribs. The impact felt like a hammer to bone: blunt, deep, and ruthless. Ayan staggered, pain flaring across his side, but he gritted his teeth and refused to go down.

Kabir was fast. Too fast. His movements were smooth, measured, and almost effortless. Every dodge, every counter was flawless. Ayan kept fighting, but nothing he did was working. Years of pain, of training, of imagined vengeance; yet none of it was enough. Kabir blocked and sidestepped every punch, every kick, without breaking a sweat.

Then came Kabir's second hit: a crushing blow to Ayan's gut. The breath left Ayan's lungs as his knees buckled. He dropped for a moment, gasping, but rage surged through him like fuel. He stood, barely steady, and threw another punch.

Kabir caught it mid-air and slammed his knuckles into Ayan's face. The impact was brutal, snapping Ayan's head to the side and sending him crashing to the ground.

Kabir stood tall above him, expression unreadable except for the faint glint of disappointment in his eyes.

"Is that all, little brother?" he said flatly. "All this time. All this training. And still... too weak.".

Ayan staggered, gasping.

He lunged again. Grabbed Kabir. For a second, they grappled. Ayan saw his brother's eyes up close: calm. Empty.

Kabir twisted. Ayan flew. Crashed against the wall.

Still, he stood.

He pushed himself up and charged again and again, fists flying, fury overriding pain. Punch after punch, he came at Kabir, wild but determined. Kabir blocked them, moving with a grace that mocked Ayan's rage. Until one strike: one furious, desperate punch slipped through.

A grazing blow to Kabir's jaw. Barely a hit, but it landed.

Kabir winced.

Ayan's breath hitched.

For the first time, a faint, bitter smile curled on Ayan's face.

Kabir smirked back, unfazed. "Well done," he said. "You almost tickled me."

They clashed again. This time, it wasn't one-sided. Ayan fought with clarity. He ducked, countered, and timed his movements. After multiple failed attempts, he broke through Kabir's defense and landed a solid punch across his face. Kabir's head snapped slightly to the side.

Ayan stepped back, chest heaving, watching Kabir crack his jaw back into place.

"Now we're talking," Kabir gave a slight nod. "Let's see what you're made of."

They launched into each other again, fists like thunder, echoing in the hollow silence of the mansion. Every strike came harder. Each block was faster. They moved like mirrors: brothers by blood, enemies by fate.

But something was shifting.

Ayan began to feel it. Kabir's timing was off. His footwork was getting slower. His dodges... just a second too late.

Then it happened.

Kabir coughed.

A crimson spray hit the floor.

Ayan paused, confused. He thought it was from his punch, but it didn't add up. Kabir's next punches lacked the same strength. His grip faltered. His stance... less balanced.

Ayan's eyes narrowed.

Something's wrong.

Kabir blocked one of Ayan's punches and swung toward his face, but a sudden cough stole the power from his strike. Blood burst from his mouth again. Ayan saw the opening and took it. He slipped past and drove his foot into Kabir's gut.

Kabir flew back, hit the floor hard, and struggled to rise.

That's when Ayan saw it... truly saw it.

Kabir was sick.

He wasn't just slowing; He was breaking.

His breathing was uneven, his hands trembling, his eyes slightly unfocused. He had masked it well... until now. Now, the cracks were visible.

Ayan felt a wave of something unfamiliar: a dull ache deep in his chest. But he shoved it aside.

He surged forward.

This time, Kabir couldn't keep up. Ayan's punches came like a storm, relentless and ruthless. A crushing uppercut to the ribs sent Kabir reeling. He stumbled back, hacking blood onto the floor. The sound echoed like thunder in the silence.

Still, Kabir stood. Still, he smiled.

"You're slipping," Ayan spat, venom in his voice. "Where's that untouchable assassin now, huh?"

Kabir chuckled, breathless. "I was wondering when you'd notice."

His voice was weaker now, thinner. But the defiance in his eyes remained. "You're finally thinking like me."

Ayan hesitated.

Kabir wiped the blood from his mouth, gazing up at his brother. "But tell me, Ayan... do you feel stronger now? Standing over your dying enemy?".

Ayan's fists clenched.

Kabir launched forward with whatever strength he had left. His fists came hard: desperate, wild, like a storm on its last legs. Ayan ducked, barely avoiding a vicious elbow aimed for his throat. They crashed into each other again, striking like meteors. But Kabir was fading fast.

Each hit Ayan landed pushed him back. Each hit Kabir threw lacked force.

Ayan drove his knee into Kabir's gut, the final blow.

Kabir collapsed.

Blood poured from his mouth as he coughed violently. He tried to rise, but his arms trembled, collapsing beneath him.

He had nothing left.

Ayan stood over him, chest heaving, fists shaking. He had won.

But Kabir... he wasn't afraid.

"He looked up at Ayan, not with fear, but with a calm satisfaction, as if everything had gone exactly the way he wanted."

"Goodbye… little brother," he whispered.

His voice was barely there, a whisper on the wind, with a smile on his face.

Ayan froze.

Everything inside him screamed: ask why, demand answers, do something.

But his body didn't move. His breath caught.

He watched as the light faded from Kabir's eyes.

And just like that… it was over.

Outside the old Yusuf Ali mansion, the storm raged on. Lightning split the sky, thunder shook the earth, and the wind howled through the shattered windows. Rain poured relentlessly, washing away the blood that stained the ground.

Ayan sat beside Kabir's lifeless body, motionless. He had done it. The purpose that had fueled him since he was seven years old had finally been fulfilled. Yet, as he stared at the unmoving figure before him, there was no triumph. No sense of peace. No closure.

Just emptiness.

His breath was heavy, uneven. Sweat and blood dripped from his face, merging with the rain as it pooled on the cold floor. His fingers trembled, his body exhausted beyond its limits. The weight of it all pressed down on him, suffocating, consuming.

His vision blurred. His body swayed. The distant sound of sirens cut through the storm, growing louder with each passing second. Red and blue lights flickered against the mansion's ruined walls.

The police patrol jeep screeched to a halt. Boots splashed through the mud as officers rushed in, their flashlights slicing through the darkness. Their eyes widened at the scene before them: Ayan, bruised and bloodied, slumped unconscious beside Kabir's body, the room a wreck of destruction.

One officer quickly pulled out his phone, calling in their higher-ups. Two others moved toward Ayan, carefully lifting his battered form and carrying him outside. The rain poured over him as they placed him in the jeep, his head lolling to the side.

Meanwhile, another officer remained behind, his gaze shifting between the broken furniture, the shattered glass, and the lifeless body of Kabir Yusuf Ali. He exhaled sharply, pulling out his radio to report back.

As the police jeep sped toward the nearest hospital, the storm raged on, relentless and unforgiving.

TWENTY-THREE
THE TRUTH

The faint beeping of the monitor was the only sound in the room. Ayan lay still on the bed, bruises lining his arms, his face pale. Near him sat Balveer, arms crossed, and Raghav, in a wheelchair...still weak, but present.

For a long time, nobody spoke.

It was Balveer who finally broke the silence.

"We heard what happened. The scene has been cleared."

Ayan didn't look up. His voice was hollow.

"And Kabir?"

Raghav took a long, painful breath.

"He's gone. The medical team confirmed it."

He paused, struggling to finish.

"They say it was internal bleeding... from the beating. But also... he..." He didn't finish.

Ayan's eyes remained fixed on the window.

"He was sick."

Raghav blinked in surprise.

"You knew?"

Ayan nodded faintly.

"He kept coughing up blood... And during the fight, his punches... they were slower. That wasn't like him."

Balveer leaned forward gently.

"How do you feel now, Ayan?"

Ayan glanced at his bruised hands.

His voice was low, confused.

"I don't know."

Raghav and Balveer exchanged a glance.

Raghav spoke softly.

"This is what you always wanted... right?"

Ayan's hands clenched. His voice cracked.

"Then why don't I feel satisfied?"

Even Raghav looked startled by that.

Then suddenly, something flickered in Ayan's eyes.

"Before you went into the ICU... you said there was a truth I deserved to know. What was it?"

Balveer sat up straighter. Raghav hesitated, looking down.

"I don't think it's important anymore," he said.

Ayan's voice grew sharper.

"It felt important then. Like it was the last thing you wanted to tell me before you died."

Balveer looked at Raghav.

"I think you should tell him."

"No, Balveer. We can't."

"The boy deserves to know. It's time."

"What is it?" he asked, his voice shaking. "What truth?"

There was a pause.

Balveer looked at him seriously, gravely.

"It's about your brother, Ayan. It's about the truth."

Ayan's brows furrowed, his voice low and serious.

"What truth? We know the truth. He was a terrorist. He killed my family. He turned his back on this country. He...

Raghav interrupted.

"No, Ayan. That's the truth he wanted you to believe. That's the truth he made the world believe."

He leaned forward, locking eyes with him.

"You think you know your brother. You don't."

Ayan stood frozen.

Raghav's voice dropped to a grave tone.

"Your family wasn't what you thought they were."

The room went silent for a moment.

"They were part of a sleeper cell. A hidden network working for Ibrahim Al-Malik's organization". Ayan's eyes widened.

"And your father... he wasn't just a businessman. He led that cell."

Ayan's breath caught.

"No..." he whispered.

"That can't be true."

Raghav took a deep breath, eyes distant, as if he were staring into a moment frozen in time.

"Kabir was fifteen... when they tried to pull him in."

His voice dropped to a softer tone.

"They saw potential in him. Intelligence. Calm. Obedience. He was everything they needed."

Another pause. His hand trembled slightly on the armrest.

"But Kabir... he wasn't like any other fifteen-year-old. He was different."

Raghav looked at Ayan, his eyes heavy with memory.

"He was a pacifist at heart. He had already seen what war looked like. The Kargil conflict left scars in his mind, images he couldn't erase: burning houses. Bullet-riddled bodies. Screams."

Raghav's eyes dimmed.

"He was a boy who thought beyond his age. Wise beyond his years. He hated it. Despised the idea of killing innocent people."

He paused.

"When he turned fifteen, he started noticing things. Secret meetings. Satellite phones. Weapons, hidden in the house. And he did the one thing he could do... he came to me."

Raghav looked at Ayan.

"One day, after class, he walked straight into my office. I thought he was just another student exaggerating something. But when he spoke... when he told me everything... I realized he was dead serious."

Balveer added, his tone deep and composed:

"Raghav called me. We didn't want to believe it at first. But the way Kabir described everything, the precision... we knew he wasn't lying."

Raghav nodded.

"But your family had a spotless image. We couldn't arrest anyone without concrete proof. So we asked Kabir to help us."

Balveer continued:

"And he agreed. Because he knew... if the truth came out, it would tear the country apart. People would start killing each other in the name of religion. Chaos would follow."

He looked at Ayan with a somber smile.

"I always admired him. A boy... carrying the burden of an entire country's safety on his back."

There was silence again.

Then Raghav said softly:

"October 7, 2004. That day, your house held a gathering. They were planning to execute three simultaneous bombings across Mumbai. On Diwali."

Ayan's world froze.

"Kabir couldn't gather all the details. We couldn't stop it. We had no choice."

Then the words came like a blade.

"Kabir executed every single member of your family... under the orders of the Indian Army."

Ayan gasped. He clutched his chest, eyes wide, breath shortening. "What... What? I...I..."

He couldn't form words. His mind was shattering.

"Breathe, Ayan," Raghav said, alarmed.

But it was too late.

Ayan was having a panic attack. Balveer gripped his shoulders.

"Look at me. Breathe... slowly... in... and out..."

It took several minutes. But eventually, Ayan's breathing steadied.

Balveer spoke gently.

"Kabir was planning to surrender that night. But... he found your father's journal near his body."

Raghav added:

"It had names. Details. Plans. Connections. Everything. It went all the way to Ibrahim."

"How could you ask something like that from a fifteen-year-old?" Ayan's voice trembled with disbelief.

Those words were sharper than blades.

Balveer looked down, shame flickering in his eyes. He had no solid explanation, only the weight of choices made long ago.

"That's not something I'm proud of, Ayan," he said quietly. "But to save thousands of innocent lives... to keep the nation from collapsing into chaos... we had to."

Ayan's voice was faint.

"Then, Why... Why would he join them then? He already... already killed everyone."

Raghav's voice turned sharp, but his words were wrapped in pain.

"To protect you."

The weight of those words hit Ayan like a punch. He stood motionless.

"What?"

"He knew that when your family's death hit the news, others from the organization would come looking for you. To turn you into their next weapon."

Balveer stepped in:

"Kabir couldn't let that happen. So he started hunting down everyone mentioned in the journal. One by one."

"After every kill, he updated us. Eventually, he found Karim Mohammad. The man with the closest link to Ibrahim."

Raghav added:

"He stayed with Karim. Learned everything about the underworld. And... he proved himself to him, which got him into Ibrahim's inner circle. He has been feeding us intel from within enemy territory... for years."

Ayan's voice shook.

"Wait... your informant... it was Kabir?"

Raghav nodded slowly.

"I don't believe you... That day, in his room. I heard him talking about guns. Blasts... on the phone."

Raghav replied gently.

"He was talking to me, Ayan."

Silence lingered.

Then, Raghav said with a heavy heart:

"Kabir killed everyone. His father. His mother. His uncles and aunts. Even your cousins. But he couldn't kill you."

Raghav looked straight at Ayan.

"Because he loved you... too much."

Ayan had no strength left. He stared at the floor, completely broken.

Raghav continued:

"He would occasionally come back. To make sure you were okay."

Balveer added softly:

"He was not happy with Siva's death. It happened without his knowledge or involvement. It was all Amar."

Raghav said:

"The day of my retirement... Kabir came to give us intel about an attack planned for the next day. The one we stopped. That day... I told him about Siva."

Ayan's jaw tightened.

Raghav finished:

"He wanted to make sure Siva was not a threat to you... In disguise. And after your confrontation, he told me something."

Raghav smiled faintly.

"He said he's glad someone like Siva is in your life. Someone... who sees you as a brother."

Balveer stood up, his voice gentle, but resolute.

"When our commandos reached the destination, they didn't find an army of men with guns and explosives," he said. "What they found was a graveyard: thirty-six dead terrorists scattered across the camp like broken dolls. And inside one of the tents... the lifeless body of Ibrahim Al-Malik. A knife driven straight through his heart."

He paused for a moment, his eyes sharp with the weight of memory.

"Beside him was a book. Not just any book. It contained everything: coordinates of their hidden bases, the names of every sleeper cell operating in India, their upcoming plans... and even the identities of high-profile Indians working with Ibrahim, backed by hard proof."

He let out a breath. "At the end of that book, written in blood, were two words...Vande Mataram"

"Ayan... your brother was a great soldier. And an even greater brother."

He stepped closer to the bed, placing a firm hand on Ayan's shoulder.

"Everything he did... every lie he let you believe, every moment he made you hate him... was to protect you. To make you strong. So that you could survive in a world where people like him... people like your father... existed."

Raghav added softly, "He carried that burden alone. Took on the image of a villain... just so you'd have a reason to rise. To fight. To stand on your own and when the time finally came... when his body gave up, when the disease took its toll, he didn't run. He came back to you. Not as a monster. But as your brother."
Ayan turned to look at him, eyes glassy with grief.

Raghav finished the thought in a whisper:
"He chose to die in your arms, in your home... where everything began."

A tear escaped from Ayan's eye as he turned to the other side. It was too much information. Too much weight all at once. Raghav and Balveer knew it would take a long time for him to take it all in.

Days later, Ayan found himself alone near Siva's tombstone at the orphanage. A bouquet of fresh flowers lay beside the grave. His eyes were filled with tears, silently streaming down his cheeks as he stared at the name engraved in stone.

Memories started to drift through him, of the brother who once protected him, who smiled like the world hadn't yet turned cruel. In the quiet, he saw Kabir again: not the man the world feared, but the boy who gave up everything. And as the wind whispered through the trees, Ayan realized some goodbyes were never meant to be understood...only mourned.

The world felt quiet. Too quiet. Just then, a small voice broke the silence.

"Ayan bhayya... someone asked me to give this to you."

He turned. A little girl stood there, holding a small brown package, no larger than a lunch tin.

"Who gave this to you?" he asked, wiping his face, confused.

She pointed toward the gate. "Someone in a black car. They didn't say anything. Just smiled... and drove off."

Ayan took the box. He placed it on the ground and opened the lid.

Ayan stared at it, eyes wide, chest rising with shallow, rapid breaths.

He froze.

Inside was a small sculpture: smooth, cold, carved with eerie precision.

A white viper.

"END OF BOOK 1"

*"Kabir lived and died a villain in his brother's eyes,
but in the shadows, he waged a silent war no soul would ever
know.
How many like him have sacrificed their names, their honor,
their very lives,
all for a cause greater than themselves?
How many heroes have worn the mask of a monster,
so the world might rest in peaceful slumber?"*